Maurice Leblanc

Arsène Lupin

Gentleman-Thief

Imprint: Independently published
ISBN: 9798734896891

Content

The arrest of Arsène Lupin..5
Arsène Lupin in prison...17
The escape of Arsène Lupin..37
The Mysterious Traveler..57
The Queen's Necklace 71
The Seven of Hearts..87
The safe of Madame Imbert 119
The Black Pearl..129
Herlock Sholmes arrives too late 143

The arrest of Arsène Lupin

It was a strange end to a voyage that had begun in a most auspicious manner. The transatlantic steamer "La Provence" was a fast and comfortable vessel, commanded by a most amiable man. The passengers formed a select and delightful company. The charm of new acquaintances and improvised amusements made the time pass quickly. We enjoyed the pleasant feeling of being separated from the world, living on an unknown island, so to speak, and therefore forced to be sociable with each other.

Have you ever thought about how much originality and spontaneity comes from these different individuals who didn't even know each other the night before and are now condemned for a few days to live a life of extreme intimacy, braving together the fury of the ocean, the terrible onslaught of the waves, the violence of the storm and the agonizing monotony of the calm and sleepy water? Such a life becomes a kind of tragic existence, with its storms and its sublimities, its monotony and its diversity; and this is perhaps why we embark on this short journey with mixed feelings of joy and fear.

But in recent years a new sensation has been added to the life of the transatlantic traveler. The little floating island is now connected to the world from which it was once quite free. A bond connected them, even in the heart of the watery expanse of the Atlantic. This ribbon is the wireless telegraph through which we receive messages in the most mysterious way. We know very well that the message is not carried by a hollow wire. No, the mystery is even more inexplicable, even more romantic, and we must resort to the wings of the air to explain this new wonder. During the first day of the journey we had the feeling that that distant voice followed us, accompanied us, even preceded us, whispering from time to time to one of us a few words from the raptured world. Two friends spoke to me. Ten, twenty others sent cheerful or somber words of farewell to other passengers.

On the second day, at a distance of five hundred miles from the French coast, in the midst of a violent storm, we received the following message by wireless telegraph:

Arsène Lupin is on your ship, first cabin, blond hair, wounded right forearm, traveling alone under the name R....

At that moment a terrible lightning flashed through the stormy sky. The electric waves were interrupted. The rest of the dispatch never reached us. Of the name under which Arsène Lupin hid, we knew only the initials.

Had it been any other message, the secret would no doubt have been carefully guarded by both the telegraph operator and the officers of the ship. But it was one of those events calculated to escape the strictest discretion. That very day, no one knew how, the incident became the current gossip and every passenger was aware that the famous Arsène Lupin was hiding in our midst.

Arsène Lupin in our midst!

The unpredictable burglar whose deeds had been reported in all the newspapers in recent months! The mysterious individual with whom Ganimard, our most astute inspector, had engaged in a relentless conflict in the midst of an interesting and picturesque setting. Arsène Lupin, the eccentric gentleman who operates only in châteaux and salons, and who entered the residence of Baron Schormann one evening, but came out empty-handed, leaving behind, however, his card on which he had scrawled these words:

"Arsène Lupin, gentleman burglar, will return if the furniture is genuine."

Arsène Lupin, the man of a thousand disguises: alternately chauffeur, detective, bookmaker, Russian doctor, Spanish bullfighter, traveling salesman, sturdy youth or decrepit old man.

Then this perplexing situation: Arsène Lupin wandering within the limited world of a transatlantic steamer; in this very small corner of the world, in this dining room, in this smoking room, in this music room! Arsène Lupin was perhaps that gentleman ... or that ... my tablemate ... the roommate of my cabin ....

"And this condition will last five days!" exclaimed Miss Nelly Underdown the next morning. "It is intolerable! I hope he will be arrested."

Then, turning to me, she added:

"And you, Monsieur d'Andrézy, you are in close contact with the captain; surely you know something?"

I would have been delighted if I had possessed any information that would have interested Miss Nelly. She was one of those splendid figures who inevitably attract attention in any gathering. Wealth and beauty make an irresistible combination, and Nelly possessed both.

Educated in Paris under the care of a French mother, she was now on her way to visit her father, the Chicago millionaire Underdown. She was accompanied by one of her friends, Lady Jerland.

At first I had intended to begin a flirtation with her; but in the rapidly growing intimacy of the journey I was soon impressed by her charming manner, and my feelings became too deep and reverent for mere flirtation. Moreover, she accepted my attentions with some degree of benevolence. She deigned to laugh at my jokes and show interest in my stories. Nevertheless, I felt that I had a rival in the person of a young man of quiet and refined taste; and it sometimes struck me that she preferred his taciturn humor to my Parisian frivolity. He was one of the circle of admirers that surrounded Miss Nelly when she addressed the above question to me. We were all sitting comfortably in our deck chairs. The storm of the night before had cleared the sky. The weather was now glorious.

"I don't know exactly, Mademoiselle," I replied, "but can't we investigate the mystery ourselves - like Inspector Ganimard, the personal enemy of Arsène Lupin?"

"Oh! Oh! You are making very rapid progress, monsieur."

"Not at all, mademoiselle. First of all, may I ask if you think the problem is complicated?"

"Very complicated."

"Have you forgotten the key we have to solving the problem?"

"What key?"

"For starters, Lupin calls himself Monsieur R. ."

"A rather vague piece of information," she replied.

"Second, he travels alone."

"Does that help you?" she asked.

"Third, he's blond."

"So?"

"Then all we have to do is look through the passenger list and use the process of elimination."

I had the list in my pocket. I took it out and flipped through it. Then I remarked:

"I find only thirteen men on the passenger list whose names begin with the letter R."

"Only thirteen?"

"Yes, in the first cabin. And of those thirteen, I see that nine of them are accompanied by wives, children, or servants. So that leaves only four who are traveling alone. First, the Marquis de Raverdan ... "

"Secretary to the American ambassador," interrupted Miss Nelly. "I know him."

"Major Rawson," I continued.

"He's my uncle," someone said.

"Mr. Rivolta."

"Here!" cried an Italian, whose face was hidden under a heavy black beard.

Miss Nelly burst out laughing and exclaimed, "That gentleman can hardly be called blond."

"Very well," I said, "then we are forced to conclude that the culprit is the last on the list."

"What is his name?"

"Mr. Rozaine. Does anyone know him?"

No one answered. But Miss Nelly turned to the taciturn young man whose attentions to her had annoyed me and said:

"Well, Monsieur Rozaine, why don't you answer?"

All eyes were now on him. He was a blond. I must confess that I myself felt a shock of surprise, and the profound silence that followed her question showed that the others present also regarded the situation with a feeling of sudden alarm. The thought was absurd, however, for the gentleman in question seemed perfectly innocent.

"Why don't I answer?" he asked. "Because, considering my name, my position as a lonely traveler, and the color of my hair, I have already come to the same conclusion, and now I think I should be arrested."

He made a strange expression as he uttered these words. His thin lips were drawn closer together than usual and his face was ghastly pale, while his eyes were bloodshot. He was joking, of course, but his appearance and bearing made a strange impression on us.

"But you don't have the wound?" asked Miss Nelly naively.

"That is true," he replied, "I lack the wound."

Then he pulled up his sleeve, removed his cuff, and showed us his arm. But this action did not deceive me. He had shown us his left arm, and I was about to call his attention to this fact, when another incident diverted our attention. Lady Jerland, Miss Nelly's friend, came running toward us in great excitement, exclaiming:

"My jewels, my pearls! Someone has stolen them all!"

No, they were not all gone, as we soon found out. The thief had taken only part of them; a very strange thing. Of the diamond sunbursts, jeweled pendants, bracelets and necklaces, the thief had taken not the largest stones, but the finest and most valuable. The settings lay on the table. I saw them there, robbed of their jewels, like flowers from which the beautiful colorful petals had been ruthlessly plucked. And this theft must have been committed at the time Lady Jerland was taking her tea; in broad daylight, in a cabin that opened into a busy corridor; moreover, the thief had been compelled to force open the door of the cabin, search for the jewel-box that was hidden at the bottom of a hat-box, open it, pick out his prey, and remove them from the settings.

Of course, all passengers immediately came to the same conclusion: it was the work of Arsène Lupin.

That day at dinner, the seats to Rozaine's right and left remained empty; and during the evening it was rumored that the captain had placed him under arrest, which brought a sense of security and relief. We breathed another sigh of relief. That evening we resumed our games and dances. Miss Nelly, in particular, displayed a spirit of thoughtless gaiety that convinced me that she had already forgotten the attentions of Rozaine that had been pleasant to her at first. Her charm and good humor completed my conquest. At midnight, under a bright moon, I declared my devotion to her with a fervor that did not seem to displease her.

But the next day, to our general astonishment, Rozaine was at large. We learned that the evidence against him was insufficient. He had produced quite regular documents showing that he was the son of a wealthy merchant from Bordeaux. Moreover, his arms bore not the slightest trace of a wound.

"Certificates! Birth certificates!" cried Rozaine's enemies, "of course, Arsène Lupin will supply you with as many as you wish. And as for the wound, he never had it, or he removed it."

Then it was proved that Rozaine was walking on the deck at the time of the theft. To which his enemies retorted that a man like Arsène Lupin could commit a crime without actually being present. And then, apart from all other circumstances, there remained one point that even the greatest skeptics could not answer: Who, besides Rozaine, was traveling alone, was blond, and bore a name beginning with "R"? Who was the telegram pointing to if it wasn't Rozaine?

And when Rozaine boldly approached our group a few minutes before breakfast, Miss Nelly and Lady Jerland got up and left.

An hour later a handwritten circular was passed from hand to hand among the sailors, stewards, and passengers of all classes. It announced that Monsieur Louis Rozaine was offering a reward of ten thousand francs for the discovery of Arsène Lupin or any other person in possession of the stolen jewels.

"And if no one helps me, I will expose the villain myself," Rozaine declared.

Rozaine versus Arsène Lupin, or rather, according to popular opinion, Arsène Lupin himself versus Arsène Lupin; the match promised to be interesting.

Nothing developed over the next two days. We saw Rozaine wandering day and night, searching, questioning, investigating. The captain also displayed commendable activity. He had the ship searched from bow to stern, rummaging through every cabin on the plausible assumption that the jewels might be hidden anywhere but in the thief's own room.

"I expect they'll find something out soon," Miss Nelly remarked to me. "He may be a magician, but he can't make diamonds and pearls invisible."

"Certainly not," I replied, "but he should examine the lining of our hats and vests and everything we carry."

Then I showed my Kodak, a 9x12, with which I had photographed her in various poses, and added, "In an apparatus no larger than this, a person could hide all Lady Jerland's jewels. He could pretend to take photographs and no one would suspect the game."

"But I have heard that every thief leaves a clue."

"That may be true in general," I replied, "but there is one exception, Arsène Lupin."

"Why?"

"Because he focuses his thoughts not only on the theft, but on any related circumstances that might serve as a clue to his identity."

"You were more confident a few days ago."

"Yes, but since then I have seen him at work."

"And what do you think about it now?" she asked.

"Well, in my opinion, we're wasting our time."

And indeed, the investigation had yielded no results. But in the meantime, the captain's watch had been stolen. He was furious. He accelerated his efforts and watched Rozaine even more intently than before. But the next day, the watch was found in the second officer's collar box.

This incident caused great astonishment and showed the humorous side of Arsène Lupin, who was a burglar but also a dilettante. He combined business with pleasure. He reminded us of the writer who almost died in a fit of laughter triggered by his own play. Certainly, he was an artist in his profession, and whenever I saw Rozaine, somber and reserved, and thought of the double role he was playing, I granted him a measure of admiration.

The following evening the officer on deck duty heard a groan from the darkest corner of the ship. He approached and found a man lying there with his head wrapped in a thick gray cloth and his hands tied together with a heavy cord. It was Rozaine. He had been assaulted, thrown to the ground, and robbed. A card pinned to his coat bore these words, "Arsène Lupin gladly accepts the 10,000 francs offered by Monsieur Rozaine. Rozaine." In reality, the stolen purse contained 20,000 francs.

Of course, some accused the unfortunate man of faking this attack on himself. But apart from the fact that he could not have tied himself up in this way, it was found that the writing on the card was completely different from Rozaine's, but on the contrary resembled Arsène Lupin's handwriting as reproduced in an old newspaper found on board.

So it turned out that Rozaine was not Arsène Lupin, but Rozaine, the son of a merchant from Bordeaux. And the presence of Arsène Lupin was once again confirmed, and in a most disturbing way.

Such fear prevailed among the passengers that no one wanted to stay alone in a cabin or move alone in unoccupied parts of the ship. People clung to each other for safety. And yet a mutual sense of distrust alienated the most familiar acquaintances. Arsène Lupin was now everyone and anyone. Our excited imagination attributed to him miraculous and unlimited power. We thought him capable of assuming the most unexpected disguises, of being alternately the highly respected Major Rawson or the noble Marquis de Raverdan, or even - for we no longer dwelt on the accusing letter R - this or that person, well known to us all, with wife, children, and servants.

The first wireless dispatches from America brought no news; at any rate, the captain informed us of none. The silence was not reassuring.

Our last day on the steamer seemed interminably long. We lived in constant fear of disaster. This time it would not be a simple theft or a comparatively harmless robbery; it would be a crime, a murder. No one could imagine that Arsène Lupin would limit himself to these two petty crimes. Absolute master of the ship, the authorities powerless, he could do whatever he wanted; our property and our lives were at his mercy.

Nevertheless, these were delightful hours for me, for they secured the confidence of Miss Nelly. Deeply moved by these shattering events and of a highly nervous nature, she spontaneously sought protection and security from me, which I gladly granted her. Inwardly, I blessed Arsène Lupin. Had he not been instrumental in bringing me and Miss Nelly closer together? Thanks to him, I could now indulge in delicious dreams of love and happiness, dreams that I sensed were not unwelcome to Miss Nelly. Her smiling eyes allowed me to continue dreaming them; the softness of her voice gave me hope.

As we approached the American coast, the active search for the thief was seemingly abandoned, and we waited anxiously for the moment when the mysterious enigma would be solved. Who was Arsène Lupin? Under what name, under what disguise was the famous Arsène Lupin hiding? And finally the great moment had come. And if I live to be 100 years old, I won't forget the slightest bit of it.

"How pale you are, Miss Nelly," I said to my companion as she leaned against my arm, almost fainting.

"And you!" she replied, "oh! You are so changed."

"This is a most exciting moment, and I am delighted to spend it with you, Miss Nelly. I hope your memory will sometimes recall it...."

But she was not listening. She was nervous and excited. The gangway was moved into position, but before we could use it, the uniformed customs officers came aboard. Miss Nelly muttered:

"I wouldn't be surprised to hear that Arsène Lupin escaped from the ship during the voyage."

"Perhaps he preferred death to dishonor and plunged into the Atlantic rather than be arrested."

"Oh, don't laugh," she said.

Suddenly I winced:

"See that little old man standing down at the gangway?"

"With an umbrella and an olive green coat?"

"That's Ganimard."

"Ganimard?"

"Yes, the famous inspector who swore to catch Arsène Lupin. Ah! Now I understand why we have received no news from this side of the Atlantic. Ganimard was here! And he always keeps his business secret."

"So you think he's going to arrest Arsène Lupin?"

"Who can say? The unexpected always happens when Arsène Lupin is involved."

"Oh!" she exclaimed, with that morbid curiosity peculiar to women, "I should like to see him arrested."

"You will have to be patient. No doubt Arsène Lupin has already seen his enemy, and will be in no hurry to leave the steamer."

The passengers now left the steamer. Ganimard leaned on his umbrella and seemed to pay no attention to the crowd hurrying down the gangway. The Marquis de Raverdan, Major Rawson, the Italian Rivolta, and many others had left the ship before Rozaine appeared. Poor Rozaine!

"Perhaps it is he after all," Miss Nelly said to me. "What do you think?"

"I think it would be very interesting to have Ganimard and Rozaine in the same picture. Take the camera. I'm overloaded."

I gave her the camera, but too late for her to use it. Rozaine had already passed the inspector. An American officer standing behind Ganimard leaned over and whispered in his ear. The French inspector shrugged his shoulders and Rozaine walked on. My God, then who was Arsène Lupin?

"Yes," said Miss Nelly aloud, "who can that be?"

There were no more than twenty people on board now. She eyed one by one, fearing that Arsène Lupin was not among them.

"We can't wait much longer," I said to her.

She walked toward the gangway. I followed her. But we hadn't gone ten steps when Ganimard blocked our way.

"Well, what's the matter?" I exclaimed.

"Just a moment, monsieur. What is your hurry?"

"I am accompanying the mademoiselle."

"One moment," he repeated in a tone of authority. Then he looked me in the eye and said:

"Arsène Lupin, isn't it?"

I laughed and replied, "No, simply Bernard d'Andrézy."

"Bernard d'Andrézy died in Macedonia three years ago."

"If Bernard d'Andrézy were dead, I wouldn't be here. But you are mistaken. Here are my papers."

"They are his, and I can tell you exactly how they came into your possession."

"You are a fool!" I exclaimed. "Arsène Lupin sailed under the name of R. "

"Yes, another of your tricks; a false trail by which you deceived them at Havre. You play a good game, my boy, but this time luck is against you."

I hesitated a moment. Then he gave me a sharp blow on the right arm that made me let out a cry of pain. He had hit the wound mentioned in the telegram, which had not yet healed.

I was forced to surrender. There was no alternative. I turned to Miss Nelly, who had heard everything. Our eyes met; then she looked at the Kodak I had put in her hand and made a gesture that gave me the impression that she had understood everything. Yes, there, between the narrow folds of the black leather, in the hollow center of the little object I had taken the precaution of placing in her hands before Ganimard arrested me, there I had deposited Rozaine's twenty thousand francs and Lady Jerland's pearls and diamonds.

Oh! I swear that at that solemn moment when I found myself in the power of Ganimard and his two assistants, I was indifferent to everything, my arrest, the hostility of the people, everything except this one question: what will Miss Nelly do with the things I had entrusted to her?

In the absence of material and conclusive proof, I had nothing to fear; but would Miss Nelly choose to provide that proof? Would she betray me? Would she play the part of an enemy who cannot forgive, or that of a woman whose contempt is tempered by feelings of indulgence and involuntary sympathy?

She passed me by. I said nothing, but bowed very low. Mingling with the other passengers, she walked to the gangway with my Kodak in her hand. It occurred to me that she wouldn't dare expose me publicly, but she might if she reached a more private place. However, when she had walked only a few feet down the gangway, with a movement of feigned awkwardness, she dropped the camera into the water between the ship and the dock. Then she walked down the gangway and was quickly lost from sight in the crowd. She was gone from my life forever.

For a moment I stood motionless. Then, to Ganimard's great astonishment, I murmured:

"What a pity I am not an honest man!"

That was the story of his arrest, as told to me by Arsène Lupin himself. The various incidents, which I will later record in writing, have forged certain bonds between us ... shall I speak of friendship?

Yes, I dare to believe that Arsène Lupin honors me with his friendship, and that he occasionally visits me out of friendship, bringing to the silence of my library his youthful exuberance, the contagion of his enthusiasm, and the gaiety of a man for whom fate has nothing but favor and smiles.

His portrait? How can I describe him? I have seen him twenty times, and each time he was a different person; even he himself once said to me: "I no longer know who I am. I can't recognize myself in the mirror anymore." Certainly, he was a great actor and possessed a wonderful ability to disguise himself. Without the slightest effort, he could assume another person's voice, gestures, and mannerisms.

"Why," he said, "why should I keep a certain form and a certain characteristic? Why not avoid the danger of always having the same personality? My actions will serve to identify me."

Then he added with a touch of pride:

"All the better if no one can ever say with absolute certainty: This is Arsène Lupin! The essential thing is that the public can refer to my work and say, without fear of being mistaken, Arsène Lupin did this!"

Arsène Lupin in prison

There is no worthy tourist who does not know the banks of the Seine and has not noticed in passing the small feudal castle of the Malaquis, built on a rock in the middle of the river. An arched bridge connects it to the shore. All around, the calm waters of the great river play peacefully in the reeds, and the wagtails flutter over the damp crests of the stones.

The history of Malaquis Castle is stormy like its name, rough like its outline. It has had a long series of battles, sieges, raids, plunderings and massacres. An enumeration of the crimes committed there would make the hardest heart tremble. There are many mysterious legends associated with the castle, and they tell us of a famous underground tunnel that once led to the Abbey of Jumieges and the mansion of Agnes Sorel, mistress of Charles VII.

In this ancient dwelling of heroes and brigands now lived Baron Nathan Cahorn, or Baron Satan, as he used to be called at the Stock Exchange, where he had acquired a fortune with incredible speed. The Lords of Malaquis, completely ruined, had been forced to sell the old castle at great sacrifice. It contained an admirable collection of furniture, paintings, woodcarvings and faiences. The baron lived there alone, accompanied by three old servants. No one ever entered the house. No one had ever seen the three Rubens he owned, his two Watteau, his Jean-Goujon pulpit, and the many other treasures he had acquired at public auction with an enormous outlay of money.

Baron Satan lived in constant fear, not for himself, but for the treasures he had amassed with such earnest devotion and sagacity that the shrewdest merchant could not say that the Baron had ever erred in taste or judgment. He loved them-his Bibles. He loved them dearly, like a miser; jealously, like a lover. Every day, at sunset, the iron gates at both ends of the bridge and at the entrance to the Court of Honor are closed and locked. At the slightest touch of these gates, electric bells ring throughout the palace.

One Thursday in September, a letter carrier appeared at the gate at the head of the bridge, and as usual, it was the Baron himself who partially opened the heavy portal. He eyed the man as closely as if he were a stranger, although the letter carrier's honest face and twinkling eyes had been familiar to the Baron for many years. The man laughed as he said:

"It is only me, Monsieur le Baron. It's not another man wearing my cap and blouse."

"You never can tell," the baron muttered.

The man handed him some newspapers and then said:

"And now, Monsieur le Baron, here is something new."

"Something new?"

"Yes, a letter. A registered letter."

The Baron lived as a recluse, without friends or business connections, and never received letters, and the one now presented to him immediately aroused in him a feeling of suspicion and distrust. It was like a bad omen. Who was this mysterious correspondent who dared to disturb the tranquility of his retreat?

"You must sign it, Monsieur le Baron."

He signed; then he took the letter, waited until the letter carrier had disappeared behind the bend in the road, and after pacing nervously a few minutes, he leaned against the parapet of the bridge and opened the envelope. It contained a sheet of paper that bore the heading: Prison de la Santé, Paris. He looked at the signature: Arsène Lupin. Then he read:

Monsieur le Baron:

In the gallery of your chateau there is a picture by Philippe de Champaigne, of exquisite execution, which pleases me beyond measure. Your Rubens are also to my taste, as is your smallest Watteau. In the salon to the right, I noticed the credenza of Louis XIII, the tapestries of Beauvais, the Empire gueridon signed "Jacob" and the Renaissance chest. In the salon to the left, the whole cabinet full of jewels and miniatures.

For now, I content myself with the items that can be conveniently removed. I therefore ask you to pack them carefully and send them to me, carriage paid, at Batignolles station within eight days, otherwise I shall be forced to remove them myself on the night of September 27; but under these circumstances I shall not be content with the above items.

I apologize for the inconvenience I am causing you, and consider myself your devoted servant,

Arsène Lupin.

P. S.: Please do not send the biggest Watteau. Although you paid thirty thousand francs for it, it is only a copy, since the original was burned in a night of debauchery under the directorship of Barras. Look it up in Garat's memoirs.

I do not care about the Chatelaine of Louis XV, as I doubt its authenticity.

This letter completely upset the Baron. Had it borne any other signature, he would have been greatly alarmed, but it was signed by Arsène Lupin!

As a habitual reader of newspapers, he was well versed in the history of recent crimes and therefore very familiar with the deeds of the mysterious burglar. Of course, he knew that Lupin had been arrested in America by his enemy Ganimard and was currently incarcerated in the Prison de la Santé. But he also knew that one could expect miracles from Arsène Lupin. Moreover, the exact knowledge of the castle, the location of the paintings and furniture gave an alarming aspect to the matter. How could he obtain this information about things that no one had ever seen?

The baron raised his eyes and looked at the austere outline of the castle, its steep rocky base, the depth of the surrounding water, and shrugged his shoulders. Certainly, there was no danger. No one in the world could gain forcible access to the sanctuary that contained its priceless treasures.

No one, perhaps, except Arsène Lupin! For him, gates, walls and drawbridges did not exist. What was the use of the most formidable obstacles or the most careful precautions if Arsène Lupin had decided to gain access?

That evening he wrote to the prosecutor in Rouen. He enclosed the threatening letter and asked for help and protection.

The answer came immediately that Arsène Lupin was imprisoned in La Santé prison, under strict guard, and had no opportunity to write such a letter, which was undoubtedly the work of an impostor. As a precaution, he had submitted the letter to a handwriting expert, who determined that, despite certain similarities, the writing did not come from the prisoner.

But the words "despite certain similarities" attracted the baron's attention; in them he read the possibility of a doubt which seemed to him quite sufficient to justify the intervention of the law. His apprehensions increased. He read Lupin's letter again and again. "I shall be compelled to remove it myself." And then there was the date set: the night of September 27.

To confide in his servants was a process contrary to his nature; but now, for the first time in many years, he felt compelled to ask someone's advice. Having been abandoned by the judicial officer of his district, and feeling unable to defend himself by his own means, he was about to go to Paris to engage the services of a detective.

Two days passed; on the third day he was filled with hope and joy when he read the following article in the "Reveil de Caudebec," a newspaper published in a neighboring town:

We have the pleasure of receiving in our city at the present time the veteran Inspector Monsieur Ganimard, who has gained a world-wide reputation by his skillful capture of Arsène Lupin. He has come here to recuperate, and being an avid fisherman, he threatens to catch all the fish in our river.

Ganimard! Ah, here is the help requested by Baron Cahorn! Who better to foil Arsène Lupin's plans than Ganimard, the patient and astute inspector? He was the right man for the job.

The baron did not hesitate. The town of Caudebec was only six kilometers from the castle, a short distance for a man whose pace was quickened by the hope of safety.

After several futile attempts to find out the inspector's address, the baron sought out the office of the "Reveil," which was located on the quay. There he found the writer of the article, who, approaching the window, exclaimed:

"Ganimard? Surely you will see him somewhere on the quay with his fishing rod. I met him there and happened to read his name engraved on his rod. Ah, there he is now, under the trees."

"The little man wearing a straw hat?"

"That's right. He's a gruff fellow who has little to say."

Five minutes later the Baron approached the famous Ganimard, introduced himself and tried to start a conversation, but failed. Then he got down to the real subject of his conversation and briefly described his case. The other listened motionless, his attention fixed on his fishing rod. When the baron had finished his story, the fisherman turned with an expression of deep pity and said:

"Monsieur, it is not customary for thieves to warn people they are about to rob. Arsène Lupin, in particular, would not commit such a foolish act."

"But ... "

"Monsieur, if I had the slightest doubt, the pleasure of recapturing Arsène Lupin would immediately place my services at your disposal. But unfortunately, this young man is already under lock and key."

"He may have escaped."

"No one has ever escaped from the Santé."

"But, he... "

"He, no more than anyone else."

"And yet... "

"Well, if he escapes, so much the better. I'll catch him again. In the meantime, go home and sleep soundly. That will do for the moment. You'll scare the fish."

The conversation was over. The baron returned to the castle, reasonably reassured by Ganimard's indifference. He examined the bolts, observed the servants, and in the course of the next forty-eight hours he was almost convinced that his fears were unfounded. Surely, as Ganimard had said, thieves do not warn people they are about to rob.

The fateful day was near. It was now the twenty-sixth of September, and nothing had happened yet. But at three o'clock the bell rang. A boy brought this telegram:

"No goods at Batignolles station. Prepare everything for tomorrow night. Arsène."

This telegram put the Baron in such a tizzy that he even considered giving in to Lupin's demands.

However, he hurried to Caudebec. Ganimard was fishing in the same place, sitting on a stool. Without saying a word, he handed him the telegram.

"Well, what about it?" the inspector asked.

"What's to be done with it? It's tomorrow!"

"What's tomorrow?"

"The robbery! The looting of my collections!"

Ganimard laid down his fishing rod, turned to the baron, and exclaimed in a tone of impatience:

"Ah! Do you think I am going to bother with such a silly story as this!"

"How much do you charge for tomorrow night at the castle?"

"Not a sou. Now leave me alone."

"Name your own price. I am rich and can pay it."

This offer baffled Ganimard, who calmly replied:

"I am here on vacation. I have no right to accept such a job."

"No one will know. I promise to keep it a secret."

"Oh! Nothing will happen."

"Come on! Three thousand francs. Will that be enough?"

The inspector thought for a moment and then said:

"Very well. But I must warn you that you are throwing your money out of the window."

"I don't care."

"In that case ... but what do we know about this devil Lupin! He may have quite a numerous band of robbers with him. Are you sure about your servants?"

"My confidence ..."

"You'd better not rely on it. I'll telegraph that two of my men are helping me. Now, go! It is better if we are not seen together. Tomorrow evening about nine o'clock."

The following day - the date set by Arsène Lupin - Baron Cahorn arranged his entire array of possibilities, cleaned his weapons, and paced back and forth in front of the castle like a sentinel. He saw nothing, heard nothing. At half past eight in the evening he dismissed his servants. They occupied rooms in a wing of the building, in a secluded place, far from the main part of the castle. Shortly after, the baron heard the sound of approaching footsteps. It was Ganimard and his two assistants - big, strong guys with huge hands and necks like bulls. After asking a few questions about the location of the various entrances and rooms, Ganimard carefully locked and barricaded all the doors and windows that could be used to enter the threatened rooms. He inspected the walls, lifted the tapestries, and finally placed his assistants in the central gallery, which was located between the two salons.

"No nonsense! We're not here to sleep. At the slightest noise, open the windows of the courtyard and call me. Watch out for the water side, too. Ten meters of vertical rock is no obstacle for this devil."

Ganimard locked his assistants in the gallery, took the keys, and said to the baron:

"And now for our post."

He had chosen a small room in the thick outer wall between the two main doors, which in earlier years had been the guard's quarters. One peephole opened onto the bridge, another onto the courtyard. In one corner was an opening to a tunnel.

"I believe you told me, Monsieur le Baron, that this tunnel is the only underground entrance to the castle, and that it has been locked for ages?"

"Yes."

"So unless there is another entrance known only to Arsène Lupin, we are safe."

He put three chairs together, stretched out on them, lit his pipe, and sighed:

"Really, Monsieur le Baron, I am ashamed to accept your money for such a sinecure. I will tell the story to my friend Lupin. He will be deliciously amused."

The baron did not laugh. He listened strained, but heard nothing but the beating of his own heart. From time to time he bent over the tunnel and cast an anxious glance into its depths. He heard the clock strike eleven, twelve, one.

Suddenly he seized Ganimard's arm. The latter sprang up, awakened from his sleep.

"Do you hear?" asked the baron in a whisper.

"Yes."

"What's the matter?"

"I was snoring, I suppose."

"No, no, listen."

"Ah! Yes, that is the horn of an automobile."

"Well?"

"It is very unlikely that Lupin would use an automobile like a battering ram to destroy your castle. Come, Monsieur le Baron, go to your post. I am going to sleep now. Good night."

That was the only alarm. Ganimard resumed his interrupted slumber, and the baron heard nothing but the regular snores of his companion. At daybreak they left the room. The castle was enveloped in a profound silence; it was a peaceful dawn at the bend of a quiet river. They climbed the stairs, Cahorn radiant with joy, Ganimard calm as ever. They heard no sound, they saw nothing to arouse suspicion.

"What did I say to you, Monsieur le Baron? Really, I should not have accepted your offer. I am ashamed."

He unlocked the door and entered the gallery. On two chairs, with drooping heads and drooping arms, slept the inspector's two assistants.

"Blimey!" exclaimed Ganimard. At the same moment the baron exclaimed:

"The pictures! The credenza!"

He stammered, choked, stretched out his arms toward the empty places, toward the exposed walls where nothing remained but the useless nails and cords. The Watteau, gone! The Rubens, carried away! The tapestries, taken down! The cabinets, robbed of their jewels!

"And my Louis XVI chandelier! And the Regent chandelier! ... And my twelfth-century maiden!"

In wild desperation, he ran from one place to another. He recalled the purchase price of each article, added up the figures, counted up his losses, nonstop, in confused words and unfinished sentences. He stamped with rage; he groaned with grief. He behaved like a ruined man whose only hope is suicide.

If anything could have consoled him, it would have been the amazement displayed by Ganimard. The famous inspector did not move. He seemed transfixed; he examined the room in a listless manner. The windows? ... closed. The locks on the doors? ... intact. Not a single crack in the ceiling, not a hole in the floor. Everything was in perfect order. The theft had been carried out methodically, according to a logical and inexorable plan.

"Arsène Lupin ... Arsène Lupin," he muttered.

Suddenly, as if driven by rage, he lunged at his two assistants and shook them violently. They did not wake up.

"The devil!" he cried. "Can this be possible?"

He bent over them and examined them closely in turn. They were asleep, but their reaction was unnatural.

"They were drugged," he said to the baron.

"By whom?"

"By him, of course, or by his men working on his behalf. The work bears his stamp."

"If that is so, I am lost - then nothing can be done."

"Nothing," agreed Ganimard.

"It's terrible, it's outrageous!"

"File a complaint."

"What good will that do?"

"It's good to try. The law has some means."

"The law! Bah! It's useless. You represent the law, and at this moment, when you should be looking for a clue and trying to discover something, you don't even budge."

"Discovering something with Arsène Lupin! But, my dear Monsieur, Arsène Lupin never leaves a clue. He leaves nothing to chance. Sometimes I think he got in my way and just allowed me to arrest him in America."

"Then I have to give up my paintings! He took the jewels of my collection. I would give a fortune to get them back. If there is no other way, let him name his own price."

Ganimard regarded the baron carefully as he said:

"Well, that is reasonable. Will you abide by it?"

"Yes, yes. But why?"

"An idea I have."

"What is it?"

"We'll discuss that later - if the official investigation is unsuccessful. But not a word about me, if you want my help."

He added, mumbling:

"It is true that I have nothing to offer in this matter."

The assistants gradually regained consciousness, with the bewildered expressions of people awakening from a hypnotic sleep. They opened their eyes and looked around in amazement. Ganimard questioned them; they remembered nothing.

"But you must have seen someone?"

"No."

"Can't you remember?"

"No, no."

"Did you have anything to drink?"

They thought for a moment, and then one of them answered:

"Yes, I drank a little water."

"From the carafe?"

"Yes."

"So did I," the other declared.

Ganimard smelled and tasted. It had no particular taste or smell.

"Come on," he said, "we're wasting our time here. You can't solve an Arsène Lupin problem in five minutes. But, for God's sake! I swear I'll catch him again."

That same day, a charge of burglary was filed by Baron Cahorn against Arsène Lupin, a prisoner in the Prison de la Santé.

The baron later regretted bringing the charge against Lupin when he saw his chateau turned over to the gendarmes, the prosecutor, the examining magistrate, newspaper reporters and photographers, and a crowd of idle curiosity seekers.

The affair soon became a general topic of conversation, and the name of Arsène Lupin so excited the public imagination that the newspapers filled their columns with the most fantastic stories about his deeds, which found instant credence with their readers.

But the letter of Arsène Lupin published in the Echo de France (no one has ever learned how the newspaper came into possession of this letter), that letter in which Baron Cahorn was brazenly warned of the impending theft, caused great excitement. The most fabulous theories were put forward. Some recalled the existence of the famous underground passages, and this was the line of inquiry pursued by the lawmen, who searched the house from top to bottom, questioning every stone, examining the wainscoting and the chimneys, the window frames and the beams in the ceilings. By the light of torches, they examined the vast cellars where the lords of Malaquis used to store their ammunition and supplies. They probed the rocky foundations to the center. But it was all in vain. They discovered no trace of an underground tunnel. There was no secret passage.

But the eager public explained that the paintings and furniture cannot disappear like so many ghosts. They are substantial, material things and need doors and windows for their exits and their entrances, and so do the people who remove them. Who were these people? How did they gain access to the castle? And how did they leave it?

The Rouen police officers, convinced of their own impotence, asked the Paris Criminal Investigation Department for help. Monsieur Dudouis, chief of the Sûreté , sent the best sleuths of the Iron Brigade. He himself spent forty-eight hours in the chateau, but to no avail. Then he sent for Ganimard, whose services had proved so useful in the past when all else failed.

Ganimard listened silently to his superior's instructions, then, shaking his head, said:

"In my opinion, there is no point in ransacking the castle. The solution to the problem lies elsewhere."

"Where?"

"At Arsène Lupin's."

"With Arsène Lupin! To support this theory, we must admit his intervention."

"I admit it. In fact, I think it's quite certain."

"Come now, Ganimard, this is absurd. Arsène Lupin is in prison."

"I admit Arsène Lupin is in prison, and closely guarded; but he must have shackles on his feet, wrists, and a gag in his mouth before I change my mind."

"Why so obstinate, Ganimard?"

"Because Arsène Lupin is the only man in France who can devise and execute such a plan."

"Mere words, Ganimard."

"But true words. Look! What are they doing? They are looking for underground passages, swinging stones, and other such nonsense. But Lupin employs no such old-fashioned methods. He's a modern thief, right up to date."

"And how would you proceed?"

"I would ask your permission to spend an hour with him."

"In his cell?"

"Yes. We became very good friends on the return trip from America, and I dare say that if he can give me any information without compromising himself, he will not hesitate to save me from unnecessary trouble."

It was shortly after noon when Ganimard entered the cell of Arsène Lupin. The latter, lying on the bed, raised his head and uttered an apparent cry of joy.

"Ah! This is a real surprise. My dear Ganimard, here!"

"Ganimard himself."

"In my chosen retreat I have felt the desire for many things, but my dearest wish was to receive you here."

"That is very kind of you, I am sure."

"Not at all. You know that I hold you in the highest esteem."

"I'm proud of that."

"I've always said Ganimard is our best inspector. He is almost - see how frank I am! - he's almost as smart as Herlock Sholmes. But I'm sorry I can't offer you anything better than this hard chair. And no refreshments! Not even a glass of beer! You'll excuse me, of course, I'm only here temporarily."

Ganimard smiled and accepted the seat offered to him. Then the prisoner continued:

"My God, how glad I am to see the face of an honest man. I am so tired of these devilish spies who come here ten times a day to rummage through my pockets and my cell to make sure I am not preparing an escape. The government is very concerned about me."

"That's quite right."

"Why is that? I would be satisfied if they would allow me to live in peace."

"With other people's money."

"Quite so. That would be so easy. But I'm only joking, and you're undoubtedly in a hurry. So let's get down to business, Ganimard. To what circumstance do I owe the honor of this visit?"

"The Cahorn affair," declared Ganimard frankly.

"Ah! Wait, just a moment. You see, I have had so many affairs! Let me first explain the circumstances of this particular case ... Ah yes, now I have it. The Cahorn affair, Malaquis Castle, Seine ... two Rubens, a Watteau, and a few trifling articles."

"Trifles!"

"All that is of little importance. But it is enough to know that the matter interests you. How can I serve you, Ganimard?"

"Must I explain to you what steps the authorities have taken in this matter?"

"No, not at all. I have read the papers and I must say frankly that you have made very little progress."

"And that is the reason I have come to you."

"I am at your complete service."

"First, the Cahorn affair was directed by you?"

"From A to Z."

"The letter of warning? The telegram?"

"All by me. I should have the receipts somewhere."

Arsène opened the drawer of a small table of plain white wood, which, with the bed and the stool, formed the entire furniture of his cell, and took from it two scraps of paper, which he handed to Ganimard.

"Ah!" exclaimed the inspector in astonishment, "I thought you were closely guarded and searched, and I find that you read the newspapers and collect postal receipts."

"Bah! These people are so stupid! They open the lining of my vest, they examine the soles of my shoes, they tap the walls of my cell, but it never occurs to them that Arsène Lupin could be stupid enough to choose such an easy hiding place."

Ganimard laughed as he said:

"What a droll fellow you are! Really, you puzzle me. But do tell me about the Cahorn affair."

"Oh! Oh! Not quite so fast! You would rob me of all my secrets; expose all my little tricks. This is a very serious matter."

"Was I mistaken in counting on your goodwill?"

"No, Ganimard, and since you insist ... "

Arsène Lupin paced his cell two or three times, then stopped in front of Ganimard and asked:

"What do you think of my letter to the baron?"

"I think you've had a bit of fun putting yourself in the limelight."

"Ah! Playing for the gallery! Come, Ganimard, I thought you knew me better than that. Do I, Arsène Lupin, ever waste my time on such childishness? Would I have written the letter if I could have robbed the Baron without writing to him? I want you to understand that the letter was indispensable; it was the engine that set the whole machine in motion. Now, let us discuss together a plan for robbing Malaquis Castle. Do you agree?"

"Yes, go ahead."

"Well, let's assume the castle is carefully locked and barricaded like Baron Cahorn's. Shall I abandon my plan and forego the treasures I covet, on the pretext that the castle in which they are located is inaccessible?"

"Obviously not."

"Shall I storm the castle at the head of a party of adventurers, as was the custom in ancient times?"

"That would be foolish."

"Can I gain entrance by trickery or deception?"

"Impossible."

"Then there is only one way open to me. I must get the owner of the castle to invite me in."

"That is certainly an original method."

"And how simple! Suppose that one day the owner receives a letter warning him that a notorious burglar named Arsène Lupin is planning to rob him. What will he do?"

"He'll send a letter to the district attorney."

"He will laugh at him because said Arsène Lupin is actually in prison. Then the simple man, in his fear, will ask for the help of the first person he meets, won't he?"

"Very likely."

"And if he happens to read in a country newspaper that a famous inspector is spending his vacation in a neighboring town ... "

"Then he'll be looking for that inspector."

"Of course. But suppose, on the other hand, that said Arsène Lupin, foreseeing this circumstance, asked one of his friends to come to Caudebec, to make the acquaintance of the editor of the Réveil, a newspaper to which the Baron subscribes, and to make this editor understand that this person is the famous inspector - what will happen then?"

"The editor will announce in the Réveil the presence of the said inspector in Caudebec."

"Exactly; and one of two things will happen: either the fish-I mean Cahorn-will not bite, and nothing will happen; or, more likely, he will run and greedily devour the bait. So you see my Baron Cahorn pleading with one of my friends against me for help."

"Original, indeed!"

"Of course, at first the pseudo-inspector refuses to render aid. Then, too, comes the telegram from Arsène Lupin. The frightened baron again rushes to my friend and offers him a certain sum of money for his services. My friend accepts the offer and calls two members of our gang who, during the night, while Cahorn is under the watchful eye of his protector, remove some objects through the window and lower them with ropes into a nice little launch chartered for the occasion. Simple, isn't it?"

"Wonderful! Wonderful!" exclaimed Ganimard. "The audacity of the plan and the ingenuity of all the details are beyond all doubt. But who is the inspector whose name and fame acted like a magnet to attract the baron and draw him into your net?"

"There is only one name that could do that - only one."

"And that would be?"

"Arsène Lupin's personal enemy, the highly illustrious Ganimard."

"Me?"

"Yourself, Ganimard. And it's really very funny. If you go there, and the Baron decides to talk, you will find that it will be your duty to arrest yourself, just as you arrested me in America. Fine! The revenge is really amusing: I'll cause Ganimard to arrest Ganimard."

Arsène Lupin laughed heartily. The inspector, very annoyed, bit his lips; to him the joke was completely humorless. The arrival of a prison guard gave Ganimard a chance to recover. The man brought lunch for Arsène Lupin, delivered from a neighboring restaurant. After placing the tray on the table, the guard withdrew. Lupin broke his bread, ate a few bites and continued:

"But, rest assured, my dear Ganimard, you will not go to Malaquis. I can tell you something that will surprise you: the Cahorn affair is about to be settled."

"Excuse me, I just saw the chief of the Sûreté."

"What about it? Does Monsieur Dudouis know my affairs better than I do? You will learn that Ganimard-excuse me-that the pseudo-Ganimard still maintains very good relations with the Baron. The latter has authorized him to negotiate a very delicate deal with me, and at the moment it is probable that the Baron has come into possession of his paintings and other treasures in exchange for a certain sum. And on their return he will withdraw his suit. So there is no longer any theft, and the law must give up the case."

Ganimard looked at the prisoner in bewilderment.

"And how do you know all this?"

"I have just received the telegram I was expecting."

"You have just received a telegram?"

"At this very moment, my dear friend. Out of politeness I did not want to read it in your presence. But if you will permit me ... "

"You're joking, Lupin."

"My dear friend, if you would be so kind as to break this egg, you would learn for yourself that I am not joking."

Mechanically, Ganimard obeyed and smashed the eggshell with the blade of a knife. He uttered a cry of surprise. Inside the shell was nothing but a small piece of blue paper. At Arsène's prompting, he unfolded it. It was a telegram, or rather part of a telegram from which the postmarks had been removed. It read as follows:

"Contract concluded. One hundred thousand bullets delivered. All in order."

"One hundred thousand bullets?" said Ganimard.

"Yes, one hundred thousand francs. Very little, but you know these are hard times ... and I have some big bills to pay. If you only knew my budget ... living in the city comes very expensive."

Ganimard stood up. His bad mood was gone. He thought for a moment, skimmed over the whole affair, trying to discover a weak point; then he said in a tone and manner that betrayed his admiration for the prisoner:

"It's lucky we're not dealing with a dozen like you, or we'd have to close up store."

Arsène Lupin assumed a modest expression as he replied:

"Pha! A man needs some diversion to fill his leisure hours, especially when he is in prison."

"What!" exclaimed Ganimard, "your trial, your defense, the interrogation - is not that enough to occupy your mind?"

"No, for I have decided not to be present at my trial."

"Oh! Oh!"

Arsène Lupin repeated emphatically:

"I will not be present at my trial."

"Really?"

"Ah! My dear monsieur, do you think I shall rot on wet straw? You insult me. Arsène Lupin will remain in prison only as long as he pleases, and not a minute longer."

"Perhaps it would have been wiser for you to have avoided coming there," said the inspector ironically.

"Ah! Monsieur is joking? Monsieur must not forget that he had the honor of making my arrest. So you should know, my worthy friend, that no one, not even you, would have laid a hand on me if a much more important event had not claimed my attention at that critical moment."

"You amaze me."

"A woman looked at me, Ganimard, and I loved her. Do you understand what that means: to be under the eyes of a woman you love? Nothing in the world was more important to me than that. And that's the reason I'm here."

"Allow me to say, you've been here a long time."

"In the first place, I wanted to forget. Don't laugh; it was a delightful adventure, and it is still a tender memory. Besides, I have been suffering from neurasthenia. Life is so feverish these days that it is necessary to take an occasional 'rest cure,' and I find this place an excellent remedy for my tired nerves."

"Arsène Lupin, so you're not a bad fellow after all."

"I thank you," said Lupin. "Ganimard, today is Friday. Next Wednesday, at four o'clock in the afternoon, I'll smoke my cigar in your house on Rue Pergolese."

"Arsène Lupin, I will be expecting you."

They shook hands like two old friends who valued each other at their true worth; then the inspector stepped to the door.

"Ganimard!"

"What is the matter?" asked Ganimard, turning.

"You have forgotten your watch."

"My watch?"

"Yes, it got lost in my pocket."

He handed the watch back and apologized.

"Forgive me ... a bad habit. Just because you took mine is no reason why I should take yours. Besides, I have a chronometer here that satisfies me quite well."

He took from the drawer a large gold watch with a heavy chain.

"Whose pocket is this from?" asked Ganimard.

Arsène Lupin glanced hastily at the engraved initials on the watch.

"J.B. ... Who the hell could that be? ... Ah! yes, I remember. Jules Bouvier, the judge who conducted my investigation. A charming fellow!"

The escape of Arsène Lupin

Arsène Lupin had just finished his meal and had taken from his pocket an excellent cigar with a gold band, which he was examining with unusual care, when the door of his cell was opened. He had just time to throw the cigar into the drawer and move away from the table. The guard entered. It was time for a walk.

"I've been waiting for you, my dear boy," Lupin called out in his usual good humor.

They went out together. No sooner had they disappeared around a bend in the corridor than two men entered the cell and began a minute examination. One was Inspector Dieuzy, the other was Inspector Folenfant. They wanted to confirm their suspicions that Arsène Lupin was in contact with his accomplices outside the prison. The night before, the Grand Journal had published these lines to its jurist:

Sir:

In a recent article you have made highly unjustified remarks about me. A few days before the opening of my trial, I will call you to account.

Arsène Lupin.

The handwriting was undoubtedly that of Arsène Lupin. Consequently, he sent letters and undoubtedly received letters. It was certain that he was preparing his escape, which he announced so arrogantly.

The situation became more and more unbearable. In consultation with the examining magistrate, the head of the Sûreté M. Dudouis himself went to the health office to explain to the director of the prison the measures to be taken. Upon arrival, he sent two of his men to the prisoner's cell. They lifted every stone, rummaged through the bed, did everything that is usual in such a case, but they discovered nothing and were about to break off their examination when the warden hurriedly entered and said:

"The drawer ... look in the table drawer. Just as I entered, he was in the process of closing it."

They opened the drawer, and Dieuzy exclaimed:

"Ah! We've got him this time."

Folenfant stopped him.

"Wait a moment. The boss will want to take inventory."

"This is a very choice cigar."

"Leave it and notify the boss."

Two minutes later, Monsieur Dudouis examined the contents of the drawer. First he discovered a bundle of newspaper clippings about Arsène Lupin from the Argus de la Presse, then a tobacco tin, a pipe, onion-skin paper, and two books. He read the titles of the books. One was an English edition of Carlyle's "Hero Worship"; the other was a charming Elzevir, in modern binding, the "Handbook of Epictetus," a German translation published in Leiden in 1634. When he examined the books, he found that all the pages were underlined and annotated. Were they intended as code for correspondence, or did they simply express the studious nature of the reader? Then he examined the tobacco box and the pipe. Finally, he picked up the famous cigar with the gold band.

"For heaven's sake!" he exclaimed. "Our friend smokes a good cigar. It's a Henry Clay."

With the mechanical movement of a habitual smoker, he held the cigar close to his ear and pressed it to make it crack. Immediately he uttered a cry of surprise. The cigar had given way under the pressure of his fingers. He examined it more closely and quickly discovered something white between the tobacco leaves. Gently, with the help of a needle, he pulled out a roll of very thin paper, barely larger than a toothpick. It was a letter. He unrolled it and found these words, written in a feminine handwriting:

The basket has taken the place of the others. Eight out of ten are finished. When pressing the outer foot, the plate goes down. Every day from twelve to sixteen, H-P will wait. But where? Answer immediately. Rest assured, your friend is watching over you.

Monsieur Dudouis thought for a moment and then said:

"It is quite clear ... the basket ... the eight compartments ... from twelve to sixteen means from twelve to four o'clock."

"But this H-P, that will wait?"

"H-P must mean automobile. H-P, horsepower, is the way they indicate the strength of the engine. A twenty-four H-P is an automobile of twenty-four horsepower."

Then he rose and asked:

"Had the prisoner finished his breakfast?"

"Yes."

"And as he has not yet read the message, as evidenced by the condition of the cigar, it is probable that he has just received it."

"How?"

"In his food. Hidden in his bread or in a potato, perhaps."

"Impossible. They only brought his food to trap him, but we never found anything in it."

"We'll look for Lupin's answer tonight. Hold him outside for a few minutes. I will submit this to the examining magistrate, and if he agrees, we will have the letter photographed at once, and in an hour you can put the letter in a similar cigar in the drawer. The prisoner must have no reason for suspicion."

It was not without some curiosity that Monsieur Dudouis returned to the prison that evening, accompanied by Inspector Dieuzy. Three empty plates stood on the stove in the corner.

"Has he eaten yet?"

"Yes," replied the guard.

"Dieuzy, please cut the macaroni into very small pieces and open the roll ... Nothing?"

"No, chief."

Monsieur Dudouis examined the plates, the fork, the spoon and the knife - an ordinary knife with a round blade. He turned the handle to the left, then to the right. It gave way and he unscrewed the handle. The knife was hollow and served as a hiding place for a piece of paper.

"Whew!" he said, "that's not very clever for a man like Arsène. But there is no time to lose. You, Dieuzy, go and search the restaurant."

Then he read the note:

I rely on H. P. to follow every day with some distance. I will go ahead.

Au revoir, dear friend.

"Well, at last," exclaimed Monsieur Dudouis, rubbing his hands in amusement, "I think we have the matter in hand. A little strategy on our part, and the escape will be a success as far as the arrest of his allies is concerned."

"But if Arsène Lupin slips through your fingers?" inquired the guard.

"We will have enough men to prevent that. However, if he shows too much cleverness, so much the worse for him! As for his band of brigands, since the chief refuses to speak, the others will have to do the talking."

And indeed, Arsène Lupin had very little to say. For several months Monsieur Jules Bouvier, the examining magistrate, had tried in vain. The investigation had been reduced to a few uninteresting conversations between the judge and Maître Danval, a leading lawyer. From time to time Arsène Lupin took the floor out of courtesy. One day he said:

"Yes, Judge, I agree with you: the robbery of the Crédit Lyonnais, the theft in the Rue de Babylone, the issue of the counterfeit banknotes, the burglaries in the various châteaux, Armesnil, Gouret, Imblevain, Groseillers, Malaquis, all my work, Judge, all my work."

"Then you will explain to me ... "

"It is useless. I confess everything in one piece, everything and even ten times more than you know."

Exhausted by his inconclusive work, the judge had interrupted his interrogations, but he resumed them after the two intercepted messages had been brought to his attention; and regularly, at noon, Arsène Lupin and a number of other prisoners were taken in a prisoner's car from the prison to the depot. They returned about three or four o'clock.

Now, one afternoon, this return trip took place under unusual conditions. Since the other prisoners had not yet been questioned, it was decided to bring Arsène Lupin back first, and so he found himself alone in the vehicle.

These prison wagons, vulgarly called salad baskets, are divided lengthwise by a center aisle from which ten compartments open, five on each side. Each compartment is arranged so that the inmate must assume and maintain a seated posture, so that the five prisoners sit one above the other, but are separated by partitions. A city guard, standing at one end, guards the corridor.

Arsène was placed in the third cell on the right, and the heavy vehicle started. He carefully calculated when they left the Quai de l'Horloge and when they passed the Palais de Justice. Then, about halfway across the Saint Michel bridge, he pressed with his outer, or right, foot on the metal plate that closed his cell. Immediately, something clicked and the metal plate moved. He was able to make sure he was between the two wheels.

He waited and kept a lookout. The vehicle drove slowly along the Boulevard Saint Michel. At the corner of Saint Germain, it stopped. A cargo horse had fallen. Since the traffic was interrupted, a large crowd of carriages and omnibuses had formed there. Arsène Lupin looked out. Another prison carriage had stopped close to the one in which he was sitting. He pushed the plate even farther away, put his foot on one of the spokes of the wheel, and jumped to the ground. A coachman saw him, roared with laughter and tried to make a yelp, but his voice was lost in the noise of the traffic that had started moving again. Besides, Arsène Lupin was already far away.

He had walked a few steps; but when he was on the sidewalk, he turned and looked around; he seemed to smell the wind like a person who does not know which direction to take. Then, having made up his mind, he put his hands in his pockets and walked up the boulevard with the carefree expression of an idle walker. It was a warm, bright autumn day, and the cafes were crowded. He took a seat on the terrace of one of them. He ordered a bock beer and a pack of cigarettes. He emptied his glass slowly, smoked a cigarette and lit a second one. Then he asked the waiter to send the landlord to him. When the host came, Arsène addressed him in a voice loud enough to be heard by all:

"I am sorry, monsieur, I forgot my wallet. Perhaps, because of my name, you will be willing to give me credit for a few days. I am Arsène Lupin."

The innkeeper looked at him and thought he was joking. But Arsène repeated:

"Lupin, prisoner at the Santé, but now a fugitive. I dare say the name will inspire your full confidence in me."

And he walked away laughing loudly, while the owner stopped in amazement.

Lupin strolled along the Rue Soufflot and turned into the Rue Saint Jacques. He continued walking slowly, smoking his cigarettes and looking in the shop windows. At Boulevard de Port Royal, he pondered for a moment and then walked toward Rue de la Santé. The high, forbidding walls of the prison were now before him. He pulled his hat forward to shade his face; then he approached the guard and asked:

"Is this the prison de la Santé?"

"Yes."

"I want to go back to my cell. The car left me on the way, and I don't want to abuse that ... "

"Well, young man, go on, quickly!" growled the guard.

"Excuse me, but I have to go through this gate. And if you prevent Arsène Lupin from entering the prison, it will cost you dearly, my friend."

"Arsène Lupin! What are you talking about?"

"I'm sorry I don't have a map with me," Arsène said, fumbling in his pockets.

The guard eyed him from head to toe in amazement. Then, without saying a word, he rang a bell. The iron gate was partially opened, and Arsène entered. Almost immediately he encountered the jailer, who gestured and feigned a fierce anger. Arsène smiled and said:

"Come, monsieur, do not play this game with me. You take the precaution of transporting me alone in the wagon, prepare a nice little obstacle, and imagine that I would turn on my heels and return to my friends. Well, and what about the twenty agents of the Sûreté who accompanied us on foot, in hackney carriages and on bicycles? No, I didn't like that arrangement. I would not have escaped alive. Tell me, monsieur, did they expect it?"

He shrugged his shoulders and added:

"I beg you, monsieur, do not worry about me. If I want to escape, I won't need any help."

On the second day thereafter, the Echo de France, which had apparently become the official reporter of Arsène Lupin's exploits-it was said to be one of his principal shareholders-published an extremely full account of this escape attempt. The exact wording of the messages exchanged between the prisoner and his mysterious friend, the means by which the correspondence was established, the complicity of the police, the walk on the Boulevard Saint Michel, the incident at the Café Soufflot, everything was revealed. It was learned that the search of the restaurant and its waiters by Inspector Dieuzy had been fruitless. And the public also learned something extraordinary that showed the infinite possibilities of the means at Lupin's disposal: the prison car in which he was transported had been prepared for the occasion and exchanged by his accomplices for one of the six cars that were on duty at the prison.

The next escape of Arsène Lupin was not doubted by anyone. He announced it himself categorically in a reply to Monsieur Bouvier the day after his escape attempt. After the judge had made fun of the matter, Arsène was annoyed and, looking firmly at the judge, said emphatically:

"Listen to me, monsieur! I give you my word of honor that this attempted escape was only a preliminary to my general plan of escape."

"I don't understand," said the judge.

"It is not necessary that you should understand."

And as the judge was about to resume his investigation in the course of this inquiry, which was widely reported in the columns of the Echo de France, Arsène Lupin exclaimed with feigned fatigue:

"Mon Dieu, Mon Dieu, what is the use! All these questions are unimportant!"

"What, unimportant?" exclaimed the judge.

"Yes; for I shall not be present at the trial."

"You will not be present?"

"No; I have made up my mind to it, and nothing will change my mind."

This certainty, and the inexplicable indiscretions that Arsène committed every day, exasperated and baffled the lawmen. There were secrets that only Arsène Lupin knew, secrets that only he could reveal. But to what end did he reveal them? And how?

Arsène Lupin was moved to another cell. The judge closed his preliminary investigation. No further proceedings were initiated in his case for two months, during which time Arsène was seen almost constantly lying on his bed, his face turned to the wall. The change to his cell seemed to discourage him. He refused to see his defense attorney. He exchanged only a few necessary words with his guards.

In the fortnight before his trial he resumed his brisk life. He complained of lack of air. Therefore he was allowed to move about in the yard every morning, guarded by two men.

The curiosity of the public was not yet extinguished; every day it awaited the news of his escape; and, in fact, he had won considerable public sympathy by his vim, his gaiety, his versatility, his inventiveness, and the mystery of his life. Arsène Lupin had to escape. It was his inevitable fate. The public expected it and was surprised that the event had been delayed so long. Every morning, the police chief asked his secretary:

"Well, has he escaped yet?"

"No, sir."

"Tomorrow, probably."

And the day before the trial, a gentleman came into the Grand Journal office, demanded to see the court reporter, threw his card in his face, and quickly left. On the card were these words:

Arsène Lupin always keeps his promises.

Under these conditions, the trial began. A huge crowd gathered in front of the court. Everyone wished to see the famous Arsène Lupin. They were in joyful anticipation that the prisoner would play some brazen tricks on the judge. Lawyers and judges, reporters and men of the world, actresses and ladies of society crowded the benches provided for the audience.

It was a dark, gloomy day with constant showers of rain. Only a dim light penetrated the courtroom, and the spectators got a very indistinct view of the prisoner as the guards brought him in. But his heavy, shambling gait, the way he slumped into his seat, and his passive, dull exterior did not seem at all inviting. Several times his advocate - one of Monsieur Danval's assistants - spoke to him, but he just shook his head and said nothing.

The clerk read the indictment, then the judge spoke:

"Prisoner in the dock, stand up. Your name, age and occupation?"

Receiving no response, the judge repeated:

"Your name? I ask you your name?"

A firm, slow voice murmured:

"Baudru, Désiré."

A murmur of surprise went through the courtroom. But the judge continued:

"Baudru, Désiré? Ah! a new alias! Well, since you've already taken a dozen different names, and this one is no doubt as made up as the others, we'll stick to the name Arsène Lupin, by which you are commonly known."

The judge referred to his notes and continued:

"For despite the most careful search, your antecedents remain unknown. Your case is unique in the annals of crime. We do not know who you are, where you come from, your birth and origin - everything is a mystery to us. Three years ago you appeared to us as Arsène Lupin, a strange mixture of intelligence and perversion, immorality and generosity. Our knowledge of your life before that date is vague and unclear. It could be that the man named Rostat who worked with Dickson, the pickpocket, eight years ago was none other than Arsène Lupin. It is probable that the Russian student who visited Doctor Altier's laboratory at Saint-Louis Hospital six years ago, and who often astonished the doctor by the ingenuity of his hypotheses on subjects of bacteriology and the boldness of his experiments in skin diseases, was none other than Arsène Lupin. It is also likely that Arsène Lupin was the professor who introduced the Japanese art of Jiu-Jitsu to the Parisian public. We have reason to believe that Arsène Lupin was the cyclist who won the Grand Prix de l'Exposition, received his ten thousand francs, and was never heard from again. Arsène Lupin might also have been the one who saved the lives of so many people through the little dormer window at the charity bazaar, and emptied their pockets at the same time."

The judge paused for a moment, then continued:

"This is the epoch which you seem to have used in thorough preparation for the war which you have since waged against society; a methodical apprenticeship in which you have developed your strength, energy, and skill to the highest possible point. Do you acknowledge the correctness of these facts?"

During this speech the prisoner had been balancing first on one foot, then on the other, with stooped shoulders and unmoving arms. Under the strongest light, one could see his extreme leanness, his hollow cheeks, his protruding cheekbones, his earth-colored face dotted with small red spots and framed by a rough, shaggy beard. Life in prison had aged and wilted him. He had lost the youthful face and elegant figure we had so often seen pictured in the newspapers.

It seemed as if he had not heard the judge's question. Twice it was repeated to him. Then he raised his eyes, seemed to think, then murmured with a desperate effort:

"Baudru, Désiré."

The judge smiled as he said:

"I do not understand the theory of your defense, Arsène Lupin. If you want to escape responsibility for your crimes because you are feeble-minded, that line of defense is open to you. But I will continue the trial, and I will not concern myself with your whims."

He then recounted in detail the various thefts, frauds, and forgeries with which Lupin was charged. Sometimes he questioned the prisoner, but he only grunted or remained silent. The questioning of the witnesses began. Some of what was testified was immaterial, others seemed more important, but through it all ran a vein of contradictions and inconsistencies. A wearying obscurity enveloped the proceedings until Inspector Ganimard was called as a witness; then interest revived.

From the beginning, the veteran inspector's behavior seemed strange and inexplicable. He was nervous and restless. Several times he looked at the prisoner, with evident doubts and fears. Then, with his hands resting on the railing in front of him, he related the events in which he had participated, including his pursuit of the prisoner through Europe and his arrival in America. He was listened to with great attention, since his capture of Arsène Lupin was widely known through the press. Toward the end of his testimony, after referring to his conversations with Arsène Lupin, he paused twice, embarrassed and indecisive. It was obvious that he was possessed by a thought he dared not express. The judge said to him sympathetically:

"If you are ill, you can withdraw for the time being."

"No, no, but ... "

He paused, looked sharply at the prisoner and said:

"I ask permission to have a close look at the prisoner. There is a mystery about him that I must solve."

He approached the defendant, examined him intently for a few minutes, then returned to the witness stand and said in an almost solemn voice:

"I declare on oath that the prisoner now before me is not Arsène Lupin."

A profound silence followed this statement. The judge, speechless for a moment, exclaimed:

"Ah! What do you mean? That's absurd!"

The inspector continued:

"At first sight there is a certain resemblance, but if you look closely at the nose, the mouth, the hair, the color of the skin, you will see that it is not Arsène Lupin. And the eyes! Did he ever have those alcohol-soaked eyes!"

"Come, come, Mr. Witness! What are you trying to say? Are you saying that we are putting the wrong man on trial?"

"In my opinion, yes. Arsène Lupin has somehow managed to put this poor devil in his place, unless this man is a willing accomplice."

This dramatic ending caused much laughter and excitement among the audience. The judge adjourned the trial and sent for Monsieur Bouvier, the jailer, and the guards who worked in the jail.

When the trial resumed, Monsieur Bouvier and the guard examined the defendant and declared that there was very little resemblance between the prisoner and Arsène Lupin.

"Well then!" exclaimed the judge, "who is this man? Where does he come from? What is he in prison for?"

Two of the prison guards were called, and both declared that the prisoner was Arsène Lupin.

One of the guards said:

"Yes, yes, I think it's him."

"What!" cried the judge impatiently, "you think it's him! What do you mean by that?"

"Well, I saw very little of the prisoner. He was placed in my care in the evening, and for two months he seldom stirred, but lay on his bed with his face to the wall."

"What about the time before those two months?"

"Before that, he occupied a cell in another part of the prison. He was not in cell 24."

Here the head guard interrupted and said:

"We moved him to another cell after his escape attempt."

"But you, sir, you saw him during those two months?"

"I had no opportunity to see him. He was always quiet and orderly."

"And this prisoner is not Arsène Lupin?"

"No."

"Then who is he?" asked the judge.

"I do not know."

"Then we have before us a man who stood in for Arsène Lupin two months ago. How do you explain that?"

"I can't."

In utter despair, the judge turned to the defendant and addressed him in a conciliatory tone:

"Prisoner, can you tell me how and since when you became an inmate of the Prison de la Santé?"

The judge's engaging manner was designed to break the distrust and elicit a concession from the defendant. He tried to answer. Finally, under skillful and careful questioning, he managed to formulate a few sentences from which the following story emerged: two months ago he had been taken to the depot, examined and released. When he left the building a free man, he was seized by two guards and placed in the prison van. Since then he had occupied cell 24. He was content there, had enough to eat, and slept well - so he did not complain.

All this seemed probable; and amid the hilarity and excitement of the spectators, the judge adjourned the trial until the story could be investigated and verified.

The following facts were immediately established by an examination of the prison records: Eight weeks earlier, a man named Baudru Désiré had slept in the dépôt. He was released the next day and left the depot at two in the afternoon. At 2 p.m. the same day, Arsène Lupin left the depot in a prisoner transport van after his final interrogation.

Had the guards made a mistake? Had they been fooled by the resemblance and carelessly mistaken this man for their prisoner?

Another question intruded: Had the exchange been arranged in advance? In that case, Baudru must have been an accomplice and arranged his own arrest to take Lupin's place. But how could such a plan, based on a series of unlikely coincidences, succeed?

Baudru Désiré was turned over to the anthropometric service; they had never seen anything like it. But they could easily trace his antecedents. He was known in Courbevois, in Asnières, and in Levallois. He lived on alms and slept in one of those rag-and-bone huts near the Barriere de Ternes. From there he had disappeared a year ago.

Had he been lured away by Arsène Lupin? There was no evidence of that. And even if it was, that didn't explain the prisoner's escape. That still remained a mystery. Of the twenty theories that tried to explain it, not one was satisfactory. Of the escape itself there was no doubt; an escape that was incomprehensible, sensational, in which the public as well as the lawmen could discern a carefully prepared plan, a combination of circumstances that miraculously fitted together, the end of which fully justified the confident prediction of Arsène Lupin: "I shall not be present at my trial."

After a month of patient investigation, the problem remained unsolved. The poor devil of a Baudru could not be kept in prison indefinitely, and to put him on trial would be ridiculous. There were no charges against him.

Consequently, he was released; but the chief of the Sûreté decided to keep him under observation. This idea came from Ganimard. From his point of view, there was neither complicity nor coincidence. Baudru was an instrument on which Arsène Lupin had played with his extraordinary skill. Baudru, if released, would lead them to Arsène Lupin, or at least to some of his accomplices. Inspectors Folenfant and Dieuzy were assigned to assist Ganimard.

One foggy January morning, the prison gates opened and Baudru Désiré stepped out - a free man. At first he seemed rather embarrassed and walked like a person who doesn't know exactly where to go. He followed the Rue de la Santé and the Rue Saint Jacques. He stopped in front of an old clothes store, took off his jacket and vest, sold his vest, for which he took a few sous; then he put his jacket back on and continued on his way. He crossed the Seine. At the Châtelet, an omnibus passed him. He wanted to get on, but there was no room. The ticket inspector advised him to get a number, and so he entered the waiting room.

Ganimard called out to his two assistants, and without taking his eyes off the waiting room, he said to them:

"Hold one car ... no, two. That will be better. I will go with one of you, and we will follow."

The men obeyed. But Baudru did not appear. Ganimard entered the waiting room. It was empty.

"I idiot," he muttered, "I forgot there was another exit."

From the waiting room, an inner corridor led to Rue Saint Martin. Ganimard hurried through, arriving just in time to see Baudru on the roof of the Batignolles-Jardin de Plates omnibus as it turned the corner of Rue de Rivoli. He ran and caught the omnibus. But he had lost his two assistants. He had to continue the pursuit alone. In his rage, he was inclined to grab the man by the collar without hesitation. Had not the supposed imbecile separated him from his assistants deliberately and by a cunning ruse?

He glanced at Baudru. The latter was lying asleep on the bench, rolling his head to and fro, with his mouth half open and an incredible expression of stupidity on his blotchy face. No, such an opponent was not capable of deceiving old Ganimard. It was a stroke of luck - nothing more.

At the Galleries-Lafayette the man jumped out of the omnibus and took the La Muette streetcar, which followed Boulevard Haussmann and

Avenue Victor Hugo. Baudru got off at the La Muette stop and strolled casually into the Bois de Boulogne.

He roamed one path after another, sometimes taking a few steps back. What was he looking for? Did he have a specific destination? After an hour he seemed to grow faint with fatigue, and noticing a bench, he sat down. The place, not far from Auteuil, on the edge of a pond hidden among the trees, was absolutely deserted. After another half hour had passed, Ganimard became impatient and decided to talk to the man. He approached and took a seat next to Baudru, lit a cigarette, drew some figures in the sand with the end of his stick and said:

"It's a beautiful day."

No response. But suddenly the man burst out laughing, a merry, cheerful laugh, spontaneous and irresistible. Ganimard felt his hair stand on end in horror and surprise. It was that laugh, that infernal laugh that he knew so well!

With a sudden movement he seized the man by the collar and looked at him with a sharp, penetrating gaze; and he found that he no longer saw the man Baudru. Certainly, he saw Baudru; but at the same time he saw the other, the real man, Lupin. He discovered the intense life in the eyes, he filled up the shrunken features, he perceived the real flesh under the flabby skin, the real mouth through the grimaces that disfigured him. These were the other's eyes and mouth, and especially his sharp, alert, mocking expression, so clear and youthful!

"Arsène Lupin, Arsène Lupin," he stammered.

Then, in a sudden fit of rage, he grabbed Lupin by the neck and tried to hold him down. Despite his fifty years, he still had unusual strength, while his adversary was obviously in a weak condition. But the fight was short-lived. Arsène Lupin made only a slight movement, and as suddenly as he had attacked, Ganimard loosened his grip. His right arm collapsed, useless.

"If you had taken jiu-jitsu lessons at the Quai des Orfèvres," Lupin said, "you would know that this punch is called udi-shi-ghi in Japanese. One second more and I would have broken your arm, and that would have been exactly what you deserved. I am astonished that you, an old friend whom I respect and before whom I voluntarily reveal my incognito, should abuse my trust in this brutal way. It is unworthy - ah! What is the matter?"

Ganimard did not answer. This escape for which he felt responsible - was it not he, Ganimard, who had led the court into a grave error by his sensational evidence? This escape seemed to him like a dark cloud over his professional career. A tear rolled down his cheek to his gray mustache.

"Oh! my God, Ganimard, don't take it to heart. If you hadn't spoken, I would have left it to someone else to do it. I could not let poor Baudru Désiré be convicted."

"Then," murmured Ganimard, "it was you who were there? And now you are here?"

"It is me, always me, only me."

"Can that be possible?"

"Oh, it is not the work of a magician. It is simply, as the judge remarked at the trial, the teaching of a dozen years that enables a man to successfully overcome all the obstacles of life."

"But your face? Your eyes?"

"You can understand that if I worked eighteen months with Doctor Altier at Saint-Louis Hospital, it was not for love of the work. I felt that he, who would one day be allowed to call himself Arsène Lupin, should be freed from the usual laws about appearance and identity. Appearance? That can be changed at will. A subcutaneous injection of kerosene, for example, plumps up the skin where you want it. Pyrogallic acid transforms your skin into that of an Indian. The juice of celandine decorates you with the most beautiful eruptions and tumors. Another chemical affects the growth of your beard and hair; another changes the tone of your voice. Add to this two months of diet in cell 24; exercises repeated a thousand times which enable me to keep my features in a certain grimace, to carry my head at a certain inclination, and to adjust my back and shoulders to a stooped posture. Then five drops of atropine in the eyes to make them haggard and wild, and the trick is done."

"I don't see how you fooled the guards," he said.

"The change was progressive. The evolution was so gradual that they didn't notice it."

"But Baudru Désiré?"

"Baudru exists. He is a poor, harmless fellow whom I met last year; and he actually bears some resemblance to me. Thinking my arrest possible, I took to Baudru and studied the points in which we differed in appearance in order to correct them in my own person. My friends induced him to stay overnight at the dépôt and leave there the next day at about the same hour as I did - an easily arranged coincidence. Of course, it was necessary to have a record of his arrest at the dépôt to establish the fact that such a person actually existed; otherwise the police would have tried elsewhere to find out my identity. But by offering you this excellent Baudru, it was inevitable, you understand, inevitable, that they should seize upon him, and in spite of the insuperable difficulties of a substitution, they would rather believe in a substitution than admit their ignorance."

"Yes, yes, of course," said Ganimard.

"And then," exclaimed Arsène Lupin, "I held a trump card: a fearful public waiting for my escape. And that is the fatal error into which you, you and the others, fell in the course of this fascinating game that hovered between me and the lawmen and in which my freedom was at stake. And you assumed that I was playing for the gallery, that I was intoxicated by my success. I, Arsène Lupin, guilty of such weakness! Oh, no! Not long ago, in the Cahorn affair, you said: `When Arsène Lupin shouts from the rooftops that he is going to escape, he has a goal in mind.' But, by God, you must understand that in order to escape, I must create in advance a public belief in that escape, a belief that is tantamount to an article of faith, an absolute conviction, a reality as glittering as the sun. And I created this belief that Arsène Lupin would escape, that Arsène Lupin would not be present at his trial. And when you made your statement and said, `This man is not Arsène Lupin,' everybody was ready to believe you. If even one person had doubted it, if someone had uttered this simple qualification: `Let's assume it is Arsène Lupin' - from that moment on I would have been lost. If someone had looked at my face, not with the thought that I was not Arsène Lupin, like you and the others at my trial, but with the thought that I could be Arsène Lupin, I should have been recognized, in spite of all precautions. But I was not afraid. Logically, psychologically, no one could have had the idea that I was Arsène Lupin."

He grasped Ganimard's hand.

"Come, Ganimard, confess that on Wednesday, after our conversation in the prison de la Santé, you expected me at your house at four o'clock, just as I had said."

"And your prison car?" said Ganimard, evading the question.

"A bluff! Some of my friends secured the old, unused car and wanted to make a try. But I thought it impracticable without the concurrence of a number of unusual circumstances. Nevertheless, I thought it wise to make this escape attempt and give it the widest possible publicity. A boldly planned escape, though not accomplished, gave the character of reality to the following one by anticipation alone."

"So that the cigar ... "

"Hollowed out by myself, as well as the knife."

"And the letters?"

"Written by me."

"And the mysterious correspondent?"

"Did not exist."

Ganimard thought for a moment, then said:

"When the anthropometric service examined the Baudru case, why didn't they realize that his measurements matched those of Arsène Lupin?"

"My measurements are not available."

"Indeed!"

"At least they are wrong. I have studied this question in detail. In the first place, the Bertillon system records the visible identifying features - and you have seen that these are not infallible - and then the measurements of the head, fingers, ears, etc. Of course, such measurements are more or less infallible."

"Absolutely."

"No; but it costs money to get around them. Before we left America, one of the clerks in the service there accepted a great deal of money to insert false figures in my measurements. Consequently, Baudru's measurements should not be the same as Arsène Lupin's."

After a brief silence, Ganimard asked:

"What are you going to do now?"

"Well," Lupin replied, "I will rest, enjoy the best food and drink, and gradually regain my former healthy condition. It is all very well to change occasionally into Baudru or some other person, and to change one's personality like one's shirt, but one soon tires of the change. I feel just as I imagine the man who lost his shadow must have felt, and I'll be glad to be Arsène Lupin again."

He walked back and forth for a few minutes, then stopped in front of Ganimard and said:

"You have nothing more to say, I suppose?"

"Yes, I do, and I would like to know if you intend to reveal the real facts connected with your escape. The mistake I made ... "

"Oh! No one will ever know that it was Arsène Lupin who was dismissed. It is in my own interest to surround myself with secrets, and therefore I will allow my escape to retain its almost miraculous character. So do not be afraid, my dear friend. I will say nothing. And now, goodbye. I am going out to dinner tonight, and I have only time enough to change my clothes."

"I thought you were going to rest."

"Ah! There are social duties one cannot avoid. Tomorrow I shall rest."

"Where are you dining tonight?"

"At the British Embassy!"

The Mysterious Traveler

The night before, I had sent my automobile down the highway to Rouen. I was to take the train to Rouen, visiting on the way some friends who live on the banks of the Seine.

In Paris, a few minutes before the train left, seven gentlemen entered my compartment; five of them smoked. No matter that the trip was short, the thought of traveling with such company did not appeal to me, especially since the carriage was built on the old model, without an aisle. I took my coat, my newspapers and my timetable and sought refuge in an adjacent compartment.

It was occupied by a lady who, at the sight of me, made a gesture of annoyance that did not escape me, and she leaned over to a gentleman standing on the running board who was undoubtedly her husband. The gentleman eyed me closely, and evidently did not dislike my appearance, for he smiled as he spoke to his wife, like one reassuring a frightened child. She smiled, too, and gave me a friendly look, as if she now understood that I was one of those gallant men with whom a woman can remain confined for two hours in a little box six feet square and have nothing to fear.

Her husband said to her:

"I have an important appointment, my dear, and can wait no longer. Adieu."

He kissed her tenderly and left. His wife threw him a few more kisses and waved her handkerchief. The whistle blew and the train departed.

At that very moment, and despite the protests of the staff, the door was opened and a man rushed into our compartment. My companion, who was standing and arranging her luggage, let out a scream of terror and fell on the seat. I am not a coward, quite the contrary, but I admit that such last-minute intruders are always disconcerting. They seem unusual and suspicious.

However, the appearance of the newcomer significantly changed the unfavorable impression that his hasty action had created. He was correctly and elegantly dressed, wore a tasteful tie, correct gloves, and his face was fine and intelligent. But where the devil had I seen that face before? For I had seen it without a doubt. And yet the memory of it was so vague and indistinct that I felt it would be useless to try to recall it at this time.

Then, as I turned my attention to the lady, I was amazed at the pallor and fear I saw in her face. She was looking at her neighbor-they were seated on the same side of the compartment-with an expression of intense alarm, and I noticed that one of her trembling hands was slowly slipping to a small traveling bag that lay on the seat about 20 inches from her. Finally, she grabbed it and nervously pulled it toward her. Our eyes met, and I read so much anxiety and fear in hers that I could not restrain myself from addressing her:

"Are you ill, Madame? Shall I open the window?"

Her only answer was a gesture that showed she was afraid of our companion. I smiled, as her husband had done, shrugged my shoulders, and explained to her pantomimically that she had nothing to fear, that I was there, and that the gentleman, moreover, seemed to be a very harmless person. At that moment he turned to us, examined us both from head to toe, then settled down in his corner and paid no further attention to us.

After a brief silence, the lady, as if she had mustered all her strength for a desperate act, said to me in an almost inaudible voice:

"Do you know who is on our train?"

"Who?"

"He ... he ... I assure you ... "

"Who is he?"

"Arsène Lupin!"

She had not averted her eyes from our companion, and the syllables of that disquieting name were addressed to him rather than to me. He pulled his hat down over his face. Was he trying to hide his excitement with it, or was he simply preparing for sleep? Then I said to her:

"Yesterday Arsène Lupin was sentenced in absentia to twenty years' penal servitude at hard labor. It is therefore unlikely that he will be so careless as to appear in public today. Besides, the newspapers have reported his appearance in Turkey since his escape from the Santé."

"But he is on this very train," announced the lady, with the evident intention of being heard by our companion; "my husband is one of the directors in the penitentiary service, and it was the stationmaster himself who told us that Arsène Lupin was wanted."

"Perhaps they were mistaken ... "

"No; he was seen in the waiting room. He bought a first-class ticket to Rouen."

"He has disappeared. The guard at the waiting room door didn't see him, and it's presumed he got on the express that leaves ten minutes after us."

"In that case they are sure to catch him."

"Unless he jumped off that train at the last moment to come here, onto our train ... which is quite likely ... which is almost certain."

"If that is the case, he will be arrested in the same way; for the clerks and guards would undoubtedly watch his passage from one train to another, and when we arrive at Rouen they will arrest him there."

"He - never! He will find some means of escape."

"In that case, I wish him bon voyage."

"But, in the meantime, think of what he might do!"

"What?"

"I don't know. He could do anything."

She was very excited, and, indeed, to some extent the situation justified her nervous excitement. I felt compelled to tell her:

"Of course, there are many strange coincidences, but you need not be afraid. If you admit that Arsène Lupin is on this train, he will not commit any indiscretion; he will be only too happy to escape the danger that already threatens him."

My words did not reassure her, but she was silent for a while. I flipped open my newspapers and read the reports on the trial of Arsène Lupin, but since they contained nothing that was new to me, I was not particularly interested. Besides, I was tired and sleepy. I felt my eyelids closing and my head sinking.

"But, Monsieur, you won't be asleep!"

She grabbed my newspaper and looked at me indignantly.

"Certainly not," I said.

"That would be very unwise."

"Of course," I agreed with her.

I struggled to stay awake. I looked through the window at the landscape and the fleeting clouds, but in a short time all this became confused and indistinct; the image of the nervous lady and the sleepy gentleman were erased from my mind, and I was buried in the soothing depths of a deep sleep. The tranquility of my sleep was soon disturbed by disturbing dreams in which a being who had played an important role bore the name of Arsène Lupin. He appeared to me with valuable objects on his back; he jumped over walls and plundered castles. But the outline of this being, who was no longer Arsène Lupin, took on a clearer form. It came toward me, growing larger and larger, leaping with incredible agility into the compartment and landing directly on my chest. With a cry of terror and pain, I woke up. The man, the traveler, our companion, was holding me by the throat with his knee on my chest.

My vision was very indistinct, for my eyes were covered with blood. I could see the lady standing in a corner of the compartment, wincing in fright. I did not even try to fight back. Besides, I didn't have the strength. My temples were throbbing; I was almost suffocating. Another minute and I would have breathed my last. The man must have noticed, because he loosened his grip, but did not take his hand away. Then he took a string in which he had prepared a slip knot and tied my wrists together. In the twinkling of an eye I was bound, gagged and helpless.

Certainly, he performed the trick with an ease and skill that betrayed the hand of a master; he was undoubtedly a professional thief. Not a word, not a nervous movement; only coolness and audacity. And I lay there, on the bench, tied up like a mummy, I - Arsène Lupin!

It was anything but a laughing matter, and yet, despite the seriousness of the situation, I appreciated the humor and irony it brought. Arsène Lupin, gripped and tied up like a novice! Robbed as if I were a simple peasant - because, you must understand, the villain had robbed me of my purse and wallet! Arsène Lupin, a victim, deceived, defeated ... what an adventure!

The lady did not move. He did not even notice her. He contented himself with picking up her traveling bag, which had fallen to the floor, and taking out the jewels, the purse and the gold and silver jewelry it contained. The lady opened her eyes, trembling with fear, pulled the rings from her fingers and handed them to the man as if to save him unnecessary trouble. He took the rings and looked at her. She fainted.

Then he calmly sat back down in his seat, lit a cigarette and examined the treasure he had acquired. The examination seemed to satisfy him completely.

But I was not so much satisfied. I am not speaking of the twelve thousand francs that had been wrongfully taken from me: that was only a temporary loss, for I was sure that after a short time I would regain possession of this money, together with the important papers that were contained in my wallet: Plans, specifications, addresses, lists of correspondents, and compromising letters. But at the moment I was preoccupied with a much more pressing and serious question: how would this affair end? What would be the outcome of this adventure?

As you can imagine, the uproar caused by my passage through the Saint-Lazare station did not escape me. Since I was visiting friends who knew me by the name of Guillaume Berlat, and among whom my resemblance to Arsène Lupin was the subject of much innocent joking, I could not disguise myself, and my presence had been noticed. So there was no question that the Rouen police chief, who had been notified by telegraph and was assisted by numerous agents, would be waiting for the train, questioning all the suspicious passengers and searching the carriages.

Of course, I had foreseen all this, but it had not worried me, since I was sure that the Rouen police would be no smarter than the Paris police and that I could escape detection; would it not suffice to carelessly show my card as a "deputy," thanks to which I had instilled full confidence in the Saint-Lazare porter? - But the situation had changed a lot. I was no longer free. It was impossible to try any of my usual tricks. In one of the compartments would be packed the Commissioner of Police Monsieur Arsène Lupin, bound hand and foot, docile as a lamb, ready to be shipped into a prison van. He should have simply accepted the package as if it were a commodity or a basket of fruits and vegetables. But what could I do to avoid this ignominious end - bound and gagged as I was? And the train sped on toward Rouen, the next and only stop.

Another problem arose, in which I was less interested, but the solution of which aroused my professional curiosity. What were the intentions of my rogue companion? Of course, if I had been alone, he could have slowly and fearlessly left the car when we arrived in Rouen. But the lady? As soon as the door of the compartment was to be opened, the lady, who was now so calm and modest, would scream and call for help. That was the dilemma that puzzled me! Why hadn't he put her in a similar helpless state as he had me? That would have given him ample time to disappear before his double crime was discovered.

He was still smoking, his eyes fixed on the window, which was now smeared with raindrops. At one point he turned, picked up my schedule and surveyed it.

The lady had to feign prolonged unconsciousness to fool the enemy. But coughing fits, caused by the smoke, revealed her true condition. As for me, I felt very unwell and very tired. And I was thinking and making plans.

The train raced on, cheerful, intoxicated by its own speed.

At that moment the man rose and took two steps towards us, whereupon the lady let out a scream of terror and fell into a real faint. What was the man going to do now? He lowered the window on our side. It was now raining heavily, and the man gestured to express his annoyance at not having an umbrella or a coat. He glanced at the rack. The lady's umbrella was lying there. He took it. He also took my coat and put it on.

We were now crossing the Seine. He rolled up his trouser legs, then bent over and lifted the outer latch of the door. Was he going to hurl himself onto the tracks? At this speed it would have been instant death. We now entered a tunnel. The man opened the door halfway and stood on the top step. What a madness! The darkness, the smoke, the noise, all gave a fantastic appearance to what he was doing. But suddenly the train reduced its speed. A moment later it increased its speed, only to slow down again. Probably repairs were being made in this part of the tunnel, forcing the trains to reduce their speed, and the man was aware of this fact. He got on the bottom step, closed the door behind him and jumped. Already he was gone.

The lady immediately regained her senses, and her first act was to lament the loss of her jewels. I gave her a pleading look. She understood and quickly removed the gag that was stunning me. She wanted to untie the cords that bound me, but I prevented her.

"No, no, the police need to see everything exactly as it stands. I want them to see what that scoundrel did to us."

"What if I pull the alarm?"

"Too late. You should have done that when he attacked me."

"But he would have killed me. Ah! Monsieur, did I not tell you that he was on that train? I recognized him by his portrait. And now he has disappeared with my jewels."

"Don't worry about that. The police will catch him."

"Catch Arsène Lupin! Never."

"That depends on you, madame. Listen. When we get to Rouen, stand outside the door and shout. Make a noise. The police and the railroad officials will come. Tell them what you saw: the attack on me and the escape of Arsène Lupin. Give a description of him - soft hat, umbrella - yours - gray coat ..."

"Yours," she said.

"What, mine? Not at all. It was his. I didn't have one at all."

"Seems to me he didn't have one when he came in."

"Yes, yes ... unless it was a coat that someone had forgotten and left in the rack. In any case, he had it when he left, and that's the essential point. A gray coat - remember! ... Ah! I forgot. The first thing you must say is your name. Your husband's official position will stimulate the zeal of the police."

We arrived at the station. I gave her some more instructions in a rather imperious tone:

"Tell them my name - Guillaume Berlat. If necessary, say that you know me. That will save time. We need to speed up the preliminary investigation. The most important thing is to track Arsène Lupin. Your jewels, remember! There must be no misunderstanding. Guillaume Berlat, a friend of your husband."

"I see ... Guillaume Berlat."

Already she was shouting and gesticulating. As soon as the train stopped, several men entered the compartment. The critical moment had arrived.

Gasping for breath, the lady exclaimed:

"Arsène Lupin ... he robbed us ... he stole my jewelry ... I am Madame Renaud ... my husband is director of the penitentiary ... Ah! Here is my brother, Georges Ardelle, director of Crédit Rouennais ... You must know ... "

She hugged a young man who had just joined us, and whom the commissioner greeted. Then she continued, crying:

"Yes, Arsène Lupin ... grabbed Monsieur by the throat while he was sleeping ... Monsieur Berlat, a friend of my husband."

The police chief asked:

"But where is Arsène Lupin?"

"He jumped off the train as it was going through the tunnel."

"Are you sure it was him?"

"I'm sure! I recognized him perfectly. Besides, he was seen at the Saint-Lazare station. He was wearing a soft hat ... "

"No, a hard felt one like that," said the commissar, pointing to my hat.

"He had a soft hat, for sure," Madame Renaud repeated, "and a gray coat."

"Yes, that's right," replied the commissary, "the telegram says he wore a gray coat with a black velvet collar."

"That's right, a black velvet collar," exclaimed Madame Renaud triumphantly.

I could breathe freely. What an excellent friend I had in this little woman.

The police agents had now released me. I bit my lips until they were bloody. I bent down, held a handkerchief to my mouth - quite a natural posture for a person who has remained in an uncomfortable position for a long time and whose mouth shows the bloody marks of the gag - and turned to the commissioner in a weak voice:

"Monsieur, it was Arsène Lupin. There is no doubt about it. If we hurry, he can still be caught. I think I can be of some help to you."

The carriage in which the crime had occurred was detached from the train to serve as a silent witness in the official investigation. The train continued its journey to Havre. We were then led through a crowd of curious onlookers to the stationmaster's office.

Then I began to have doubts. Under some pretext, I had to get my car and flee. It was dangerous to stay here. Something might happen, for example, a telegram from Paris, and I would be lost.

Yes, but what about my thief? Left to myself, in a strange place, I could not hope to catch him.

"Bah! I must try," I said to myself. "It may be a difficult game, but it's amusing, and the stakes are worth the effort."

And when the commissioner asked us to repeat the story of the robbery, I exclaimed:

"Monsieur, really, Arsène Lupin has beaten us to it. My automobile is waiting in the courtyard. If you would be so kind as to use it, we can try ... "

The commissar smiled and replied:

"The idea is good, so good that it is already being put into practice. Two of my men have set out on bicycles. They have been gone for some time."

"Where did they go?"

"To the entrance of the tunnel. There they will gather evidence, secure witnesses, and set out on the trail of Arsène Lupin."

I couldn't help shrugging my shoulders as I replied:

"Your men will not be securing evidence or witnesses."

"Really?"

"Arsène Lupin won't let anyone see him come out of the tunnel. He will take the first road ... "

"To Rouen, where we will arrest him."

"He won't go to Rouen."

"Then he will stay nearby, where his arrest is even safer."

"He will not stay nearby."

"Oh! Oh! And where will he hide?"

I looked at my watch and said:

"At this moment Arsène Lupin is loitering at the Darnétal station. At ten fifty, that is, in twenty-two minutes, he will take the train that goes from Rouen to Amiens."

"Do you believe that? How do you know that?"

"Oh! It is quite simple. While we were in the carriage, Arsène Lupin was looking at my train plans. Why did he do that? Wasn't there another railroad line far from where he disappeared, a station on that line, and a train that stopped at that station? When I checked my train schedules, I found that this was the case."

"Really, sir," said the commissioner, "that is a wonderful deduction. I congratulate you on your skill."

I was now convinced that I had made a mistake in displaying so much cleverness. The commissioner looked at me with astonishment, and I thought a slight suspicion had entered his official mind ... but the photographs circulated by the police authorities were too imperfect; they showed an Arsène Lupin so different from the one he had before him that he could not possibly recognize me from them. But still he was worried, confused, and restless.

"My God! nothing excites the mind so much as the loss of a wallet and the desire to recover it. And it seems to me that if you will give me two of your men, we shall be able ..."

"Oh! I beg you, Monsieur Commissary," cried Madame Renaud, "listen to Monsieur Berlat."

The intervention of my excellent friend was decisive. Pronounced by her, the wife of an influential official, the name Berlat really became my own and gave me an identity that no mere suspicion could affect. The commissar rose and said:

"Believe me, Monsieur Berlat, I shall be glad if you succeed. I am as interested as you are in the arrest of Arsène Lupin."

He accompanied me to the automobile and introduced me to two of his men, Honoré Massol and Gaston Delivet, who were to assist me. My chauffeur cranked the car and I took my place at the wheel. A few seconds later, we left the station. I was saved.

I must confess that as I rolled along the boulevards that surrounded the old Norman town, I felt a deep sense of pride in my fast, thirty-five horsepower Moreau-Lepton, and the engine responded sympathetically to my joy. To right and left, the trees flew past us with amazing speed, and I, free, out of danger, had only to settle my little personal affairs with the two honest representatives of the Rouen police who sat behind me. Arsène Lupin was on the lookout for Arsène Lupin!

Humble guardians of social order - Gaston Delivet and Honoré Massol - how valuable was your help! What would I have done without you? Without you, I would have taken the wrong road at many crossroads! Without you, Arsène Lupin would have made a mistake and the other would have escaped!

But the end had not come yet. Far from it. I still had to catch the thief and recover the stolen papers. Under no circumstances were my two henchmen allowed to see the papers, let alone take them. This was a point that could cause me some difficulties.

We reached Darnétal three minutes after the train had left. I did have the consolation of learning that a man wearing a gray coat with a black velvet collar had taken the train at the station. He had bought a second-class ticket to Amiens. Certainly, my debut as a policeman was promising.

Delivet said to me:

"The train is an express, and the next stop is Montérolier-Buchy in nineteen minutes. If we don't get there before Arsène Lupin, he can go on to Amiens or change trains to Clères and reach Dieppe or Paris from there."

"How far is it to Montérolier?"

"Twenty-three kilometers."

"Twenty-three kilometers in nineteen minutes ... We will be there before him."

We were on the road again! Never had my faithful Moreau-Lepton responded to my impatience with such fervor and regularity. He sympathized with my restlessness. He supported my determination. He understood my hostility toward that villainous Arsène Lupin. The scoundrel! The traitor!

"Go to the right," cried Delivet, "then to the left."

We were literally flying, barely touching the ground. The milestones looked like small, frightened beasts that disappeared at our approach. Suddenly, at a bend in the road, we saw a swirl of smoke. It was the Northern Express. For a kilometer it was a fight, side by side, but an unequal fight, in which the result was decided. We won the race by twenty lengths.

In three seconds we were on the platform, standing in front of the second class carriages. The doors were opened and some passengers got off, but not my thief. We searched the compartments. No sign of Arsène Lupin.

"Jesus Christ!" - I exclaimed, "He must have recognized me in the automobile when we were riding side by side, and he jumped off the train."

"Ah! There he is now! He's crossing the tracks."

I took up the pursuit of the man, followed by my two followers, or rather by one of them, for the other, Massol, proved to be a runner of extraordinary speed and endurance. In a few moments he made up much distance to the fugitive. The man noticed it, jumped over a hedge, darted across a meadow and entered a dense copse. When we reached this copse, Massol was waiting for us. He went no further for fear of losing us.

"Quite so, my dear friend," I said. "After such a run, our victim must be out of breath. We will catch up with him now."

I examined the surroundings with the thought of proceeding alone in arresting the fugitive, in order to recover my papers, about which the authorities would doubtless ask many unpleasant questions. Then I returned to my companions and said:

"It is all very simple. You, Massol, take your place on the left, you, Delivet, on the right. From there you can watch the whole back line of the grove, and he cannot escape without you seeing him, except through this gap, and I will watch it. If he doesn't come out voluntarily, I will go in and chase him out to one or the other of you. All you have to do is wait. Ah! I forgot: in case I need you, a pistol shot."

Massol and Delivet went to their respective posts. As soon as they had disappeared, I entered the grove with the greatest caution, so as not to be seen or heard. I came upon dense brush through which narrow paths had been cut, but the overhanging branches forced me to assume a stooping posture. One of these paths led to a clearing where I spotted footsteps on the wet grass. I followed them; they led me to the foot of a hill on which stood an abandoned, dilapidated hut.

"That must be where he is," I said to myself. "It is a well-chosen retreat."

Cautiously, I crept to the side of the building. A soft sound told me he was there, and then I saw him through an opening. His back was toward me. In two steps I was with him. He was trying to fire a revolver he held in his hand. But he had no time. I threw him to the ground in such a way that his arms were under him, twisted and helpless, while I held him with my knee on his chest.

"Listen, my boy," I whispered in his ear. "I am Arsène Lupin. You will immediately and formally hand over my wallet and the lady's jewels, and in return I will save you from the police and take you into my circle of friends. One word: yes or no?"

"Yes," he murmured.

"Very good. Your escape this morning was well planned. I congratulate you."

I rose. He fumbled in his pocket, pulled out a large knife, and tried to hit me with it.

"Moron!" I exclaimed.

With one hand I parried the attack, with the other I gave him a sharp blow on the carotid artery. He fell - stunned!

In my wallet I found my papers and banknotes. Out of curiosity, I took his. On an envelope addressed to him, I read his name: Pierre Onfrey. This startled me. Pierre Onfrey, the murderer from Rue Lafontaine in Auteuil! Pierre Onfrey, who had slit the throats of Madame Delbois and her two daughters. I bent over him. Yes, these were the trains that had awakened in the compartment the memory of a face in me that I could not remember at the time.

But time was passing. I put two 100-franc bills in an envelope, along with a card that read, "Arsène Lupin to his esteemed colleagues Honoré Massol and Gaston Delivet, as a small token of his gratitude."

I placed it in a conspicuous place in the room where they would be sure to find it. Next to it I placed Madame Renaud's handbag. Why couldn't I give it back to the lady who had befriended me? I must confess that I had taken everything of interest or value from it. But, you know, business is business. And then, really, her husband is engaged in such a dishonorable profession!

The man came around. What was I to do? I could neither save him nor condemn him. So I took his revolver and fired a shot in the air.

"The other two will come and take care of his case," I said to myself as I hurried away on my way out of the woods. Twenty minutes later I was sitting in my automobile.

At four o'clock I telegraphed my friends in Rouen that an unexpected event would prevent me from making my promised visit. Between you and me, in view of what my friends must now know, my visit is indefinitely postponed. A cruel disappointment for them!

At six o'clock I was in Paris. The evening papers informed me that Pierre Onfrey had finally been captured.

The next day - let us not disdain the advantages of clever publicity - the Echo de France published the following sensational report:

"Yesterday, near Buchy, after numerous exciting incidents, Arsène Lupin succeeded in arresting Pierre Onfrey. The murderer from the Rue Lafontaine had robbed Madame Renaud, the wife of the director in the penitentiary, in a railroad carriage on the Paris-Havre line. Arsène Lupin returned Madame Renaud's handbag, which contained her jewels, and generously compensated the two policemen who had helped him in this dramatic arrest."

The Queen's Necklace

Two or three times a year, on occasions of exceptional importance, such as the balls at the Austrian Embassy or the soirees of Lady Billingstone, the Countess de Dreux-Soubise wore on her white shoulders the "Queen's Necklace."

It was indeed the famous necklace, the legendary necklace that the court jewelers Böhmer and Bossange had made for Madame Du Barry; the true necklace that the Cardinal de Rohan-Soubise intended to give to Marie-Antoinette, Queen of France; and the same that the adventuress Jeanne de Valois, Countess de la Motte, had torn to pieces one evening in February 1785 with the help of her husband and her accomplice, Rétaux de Villette.

To tell the truth, the mount alone was authentic. Rétaux de Villette had kept it, while the Count de la Motte and his wife scattered to the winds the beautiful stones so carefully selected by Böhmer. He later sold the setting to Gaston de Dreux-Soubise, nephew and heir of the Cardinal, who bought back the few diamonds that remained in the possession of the English jeweler Jeffreys, supplemented them with other stones of equal size but of much lesser quality, and thus restored the wonderful necklace to the form in which it had come from the hands of Böhmer and Bossange.

For almost a century, the House of Dreux-Soubise had been proud to own this historic jewel. Although adverse circumstances had greatly reduced their fortune, they preferred to cut their household expenses rather than part with this relic of royalty. The present count, in particular, clung to it like a man to his ancestral home. As a precaution, he had rented a safe deposit box from Crédit Lyonnais, where he kept it. He himself fetched it on the afternoon of the day his wife wanted to wear it, and he himself carried it back the next morning.

That evening, at the reception at the Palais de Castille, the Countess had a remarkable success, and King Christian, in whose honor the party was held, praised her grace and beauty. The thousand facets of the diamond sparkled and shone like flames of fire around her shapely neck and shoulders, and it is safe to say that no one but she could have carried the weight of such an ornament with so much ease and grace.

This was a double triumph, and the Count de Dreux was delighted when they returned to their chamber in the old house of the Faubourg Saint-Germain. He was proud of his wife and perhaps equally proud of the necklace that had added luster to his noble house for generations. His wife also looked at the necklace with an almost childlike vanity, and not without regret she took it from her shoulders and handed it to her husband, who admired it as passionately as if he had never seen it before. Then he placed it in its case of red leather, which bore the Cardinal's coat of arms, and went into an adjoining room, which was merely an alcove or cabinet separated from her chamber, and which could only be entered by a door at the foot of her bed. As on previous occasions, he hid it on a high shelf among hat boxes and piles of laundry. He closed the door and withdrew.

The next morning he got up around nine o'clock, as he wanted to go to Crédit Lyonnais before breakfast. He dressed, had a cup of coffee, and went to the stables to give his instructions. The condition of one of the horses worried him and he examined it a little more closely in the yard. Then he returned to his wife, who had not yet left the chamber. Her maid was doing her hair. When her husband entered, she asked:

"Are you going out?"

"Yes, as far as the bank."

"Of course. That's smart."

He entered the closet, but after a few seconds asked, without a sign of astonishment:

"Did you take it, my dear?"

"What? No, I didn't take anything."

"You must have taken it, though."

"Not at all. I didn't even open the door."

He appeared bewildered at the door, stammering in a barely intelligible voice:

"You didn't ... It wasn't you? ... Then ... "

She rushed to his aid, and together they searched everything, throwing the boxes on the floor and overturning the piles of laundry. Then the Count, rather discouraged, said:

"It is useless to search further. I put it here, on this shelf."

"You must be mistaken."

"No, no, it was on this shelf - nowhere else."

They lit a candle, as the room was quite dark, and then carried out all the linen and other articles that were in the room. And when the room was emptied, they confessed in despair that the famous necklace had disappeared. Without wasting time with futile complaints, the Countess notified the Chief of Police, Monsieur Valorbe, who came immediately and, having heard their story, inquired of the Count:

"Are you sure that no one passed through your chamber during the night?"

"Absolutely sure, for I am a very light sleeper. Besides, the chamber door was locked, and I remember unlocking it this morning when my wife rang for her maid."

"And there is no other entrance to the cabinet?"

"No."

"No windows?"

"Yes, but it is locked."

"I'll take a look."

Candles were lighted, and Monsieur Valorbe at once noticed that the lower half of the window was covered by a cabinet, which, however, was so narrow that it did not touch the casement on either side.

"Where does this window open to?"

"To a small courtyard."

"And above that you have another story?"

"Two; but at the servant's level there is a close grating over the courtyard. That's why this room is so dark."

When they moved the closet, they found that the window was locked, which would not have been the case if someone had entered that way.

"Unless," said the Count, "they went out through our chamber."

"In that case you would have found the door unlocked."

The commissioner thought for a moment, then asked the countess:

"Did any of your servants know that you were wearing the necklace last night?"

"Certainly; I did not conceal it. But no one knew it was hidden in that closet."

"No one?"

"No one ... unless ..."

"Be quite sure, madam, because it is a very important point."

She turned to her husband and said:

"I was thinking of Henriette."

"Henriette? She didn't know where we were keeping it."

"Are you sure?"

"Who is this Henriette woman?" asked Mr. Valorbe.

"A schoolmate who was disowned by her family for marrying below her station. After her husband died, I made an apartment for her and her son in this house. She is handy with a needle and has done some work for me."

"On what floor does she live?"

"On the same one as us ... at the end of the hall ... and I think ... the window of her kitchen ..."

"It opens onto this little courtyard, doesn't it?"

"Yes, right across from ours."

Monsieur Valorbe then asked to see Henriette. They went to her apartment; she was sewing while her son Raoul, about six years old, sat next to her reading. The commissar was astonished to see the wretched apartment that had been provided for the woman. It consisted of one room without a fireplace and a very small room that served as a kitchen. The commissioner continued to question her. She seemed overwhelmed when she learned of the theft. The previous evening she herself had dressed the Countess and placed the necklace on her shoulders.

"Good God!" she exclaimed, "this can't be possible!"

"And you have no idea? Not the slightest suspicion? Is it possible that the thief has come through your room?"

She laughed heartily, for she had never thought that she could be an object of suspicion.

"But I have not left my room. I never go out. And perhaps you didn't see it?"

She opened the kitchen window and said:

"Look, it's at least three meters to the ledge of the opposite window."

"Who told you the theft was committed this way?"

"But ... the necklace was in the closet, wasn't it?"

"How do you know that?"

"Well, I always knew it was kept there at night. It had been mentioned in my presence."

Her face, though still young, bore unmistakable marks of sorrow and resignation. And now it took on an expression of apprehension, as if some danger threatened her. She drew her son close to her. The child took her hand and kissed it tenderly.

When they were alone again, the count said to the commissar:

"I don't suppose you suspect Henriette. I can vouch for her. She is honesty itself."

"I quite agree with you," replied Monsieur Valorbe. "At the most, I thought there might have been some unconscious complicity. But I must confess that even this theory must be abandoned, as it does not help to solve the problem we now face."

The commissioner abandoned the investigation, which was now taken up and completed by the investigating judge. He questioned the servants, examined the condition of the latch, experimented with opening and closing the closet window, and explored the small courtyard from top to bottom. All was to no avail. The latch was intact. The window could not be opened or closed from the outside.

The inquiries concerned Henriette above all, for they were directed in her direction in spite of everything. They made a thorough investigation of her past life and found that she had left the house only four times in the last three years, and her business was satisfactorily explained on those occasions. In fact, she had been working as a maid and seamstress for the Countess, who treated her with great severity and even harshness.

At the end of a week, the examining magistrate had received no more accurate information than the police commissioner. The judge said:

"Assuming we know the culprit, which we do not, we are faced with the fact that we do not know how the theft was committed. We are confronted with two obstacles: a door and a window - both closed and locked. So it is a double mystery. How could someone get in, and how could someone escape, leaving behind a locked door and a locked window?"

At the end of four months, the judge's secret opinion was that the count and countess, who were in need of money, which was their normal state, had sold the queen's necklace. He stopped the investigation.

The loss of the famous jewel was a heavy blow to the Dreux-Soubise. Since their credit was no longer supported by a reserve that such a treasure represented, they were faced with demanding creditors and moneylenders. They were forced to sell or mortgage everything that had economic value. In short, it would have been their ruin if two large bequests from some distant relatives had not saved them.

Their pride also suffered a decline, as if they had lost a quarter of their coat of arms. And strangely enough, it was her former schoolmate Henriette on whom the Countess vented her wrath. Towards her the Countess showed the most spiteful feelings and even accused her openly. Henriette was first banished to the servants' quarters and then dismissed.

For some time the count and the countess led an uneventful life. They traveled a lot. During this time, there was only one event that went down in history. A few months after Henriette's departure, the Countess was surprised to receive and read the following letter signed by Henriette:

Madame,

I do not know how to thank you; for surely it was you who sent me this? It could not have been anyone else. No one but you knows where I live. If I have made a mistake, excuse me, and accept my sincere thanks for your past favors ....

What was the meaning of the letter? The Countess's present or past favors consisted mainly of injustice and neglect. So why this letter of thanks?

When Henriette was asked for an explanation, she replied that she had received a letter in the mail, enclosing two banknotes of a thousand francs each. The envelope she enclosed with her reply bore the Paris postmark and was addressed with an obviously disguised handwriting. Now where had these two thousand francs come from? Who had sent them? And why had they been sent?

Twelve months later Henriette received a similar letter and a similar sum. And a third time; and a fourth time; and each year for a period of six years, with the difference that in the fifth and sixth year the sum was doubled. There was another difference: after the postal authorities had confiscated one of the letters on the pretext that it was not registered, the last two letters were duly sent according to postal regulations, the first dated at Saint-Germain, the other at Suresnes. The scribe signed the first "Anquety" and the other "Péchard." The addresses he gave were wrong.

At the end of six years, Henriette died and the mystery remained unsolved.

All these events are known to the public. The case was one of those that aroused public interest, and it was a strange coincidence that this necklace, which had caused such a great stir in France at the end of the eighteenth century, should cause a similar stir a century later. But what I am about to relate is known only to those directly concerned and to a few others from whom the Count required a promise of secrecy. Since it is probable that this promise will one day be broken, I do not hesitate to tear the veil and thus reveal the key to the mystery and an explanation of the letter published two days ago in the morning papers; an extraordinary letter which, if at all possible, magnified the mists and shadows that shroud this inscrutable drama.

Five days ago a number of guests dined with the Count de Dreux-Soubise. There were several ladies present, including his two nieces and his cousin, and the following gentlemen: the president of Essaville, the deputy Bochas, the knight Floriani, whom the count had met in Sicily, and General Marquis de Rouzières, an old classmate.

After the meal, coffee was served by the ladies, who gave the gentlemen permission to smoke their cigarettes, provided they did not leave the salon. The conversation was general, and finally one of the guests happened to mention famous crimes. This gave the Marquis de Rouzières, who loved to tease the Count, the opportunity to mention the affair of the Queen's necklace, a subject that was repugnant to the Count.

Each expressed his own opinion on the matter; and of course their various theories were not only contradictory, but impossible.

"And you, Monsieur," said the Countess to Floriani, "what is your opinion?"

"Oh! I - I have no opinion, madame."

All the guests protested; for the knight had previously related in an entertaining manner various adventures which he had had with his father, a magistrate at Palermo.

"I admit," he said, "that I have sometimes succeeded in solving mysteries which the cleverest detectives have not thought of; yet I do not claim to be Herlock Sholmes. Besides, I know very little about the affair of the Queen's necklace."

All now turned to the earl, who was thus compelled to relate all the circumstances connected with the theft. The knight listened, thought, asked a few questions, and said:

"It is very strange ... at first sight the problem seems to be a very simple one."

The count shrugged his shoulders. The others stepped closer to the count, who continued in a dogmatic tone:

"To find the perpetrator of a crime or theft, it is usually necessary to determine how the crime or theft was committed, or at least how it could have been committed. In the present case, nothing is simpler, because we are not dealing with several theories, but with one positive fact, namely: the thief could only enter through the chamber door or window. Now a person cannot open a locked door from the outside. Therefore, he must have entered through the window."

"But it was closed and locked, and we also found it locked," the count explained.

"To do that," Floriani continued, paying no attention to the interruption, "he simply had to erect a board or ladder between the kitchen balcony and the window ledge, and since the jewelry box ... "

"But I repeat, the window was locked," the Count exclaimed impatiently.

This time Floriani was forced to answer. He did so with the greatest calm, as if the objection were the most insignificant matter in the world.

"I admit that it was so; but is there not a cross-beam in the upper part of the window?"

"How do you know?"

"In the first place, it was common in houses of that period; and in the second place, the theft cannot be explained without such a transom."

"Yes, there is one, but it was closed, just like the window. That's why we didn't pay attention to it."

"That was a mistake, because if you had examined it, you would have found that it was open."

"But how?"

"I suppose that, like all the others, it is opened by a wire which has a ring at the lower end."

"Yes, but I don't see–"

"Well, through a hole in the window, a person could use an instrument, say a poker with a hook on the end, to grab the ring, pull it down, and open the latch."

The Count laughed and said:

"Excellent! excellent! Your plan is very cleverly constructed, but you overlook one thing, monsieur, there is no hole in the window."

"There was a hole."

"Nonsense, we would have seen it."

"To see it, you have to look for it, and nobody looked for it. The hole is there; it has to be there, on the side of the window, in the window putty. In a vertical direction, of course."

The count rose. He was very excited. He walked nervously up and down the room two or three times, then turned to Floriani and said:

"No one has been in this room since; nothing has been changed."

"Very well, monsieur, you can easily convince yourself that my explanation is correct."

"It does not agree with the facts as found by the examining magistrate. You saw nothing, and yet you contradict everything we have seen and everything we know."

Floriani paid no attention to the count's petulance. He simply smiled and said:

"My God, monsieur, I am only putting forward my theory; that is all. If I am wrong, you can easily prove it."

"I will do that at once ... I confess that your description ... "

The Count murmured a few more words, then suddenly hurried to the door and went out. In his absence not a word was spoken, and this profound silence gave the situation an almost tragic significance. Finally the count returned. He was pale and nervous. He said to his friends in a trembling voice:

"I beg your pardon ... the revelations of the knight were so unexpected ... I never thought ... "

His wife asked him:

"Speak ... what is the matter?"

He stammered, "The hole is there, right there, on the side of the window ..."

He grabbed the knight's arm and said to him in a commanding tone:

"Now, monsieur, proceed. I admit that you are right so far, but now ... that is not all ... go on ... tell us the rest of the matter."

Floriani gently released his arm and, after a moment, continued:

"Well, here's what happened, in my opinion. The thief, knowing that the Countess would wear the necklace that evening, had prepared the board or a ladder during your absence. He watched you through the window and saw you hide the necklace. Afterwards he made the hole and pulled out the ring."

"Ah! But the distance was so great that it was impossible for him to reach the window attachment through the crossbar."

"Well, if he couldn't open the window through the crossbeam, he must have crawled through the crossbeam."

"Impossible, it's too small. No human could crawl through it."

"Then it wasn't a human," Floriani declared.

"What?"

"If the transom is too small to let a man through, it must have been a child."

"A child!"

"Didn't you say your friend Henriette had a son?"

"Yes; a son named Raoul."

"Then in all probability it was Raoul who committed the theft."

"What proof have you of that?"

"What evidence! A lot of it ... for example ... "

He paused, thought for a moment, then continued:

"For example, this board or a ladder. It's unlikely that the child could have brought it in from outside the house and carried it away without being observed. It must have used something that was nearby. In the small room Henriette used as a kitchen, weren't there some shelves on the wall where she put her pans and dishes?"

"Two shelves, if I remember correctly."

"Are you sure these shelves are really attached to the wooden brackets that support them? Because if not, we might assume that the child removed them, screwed them together, and thus formed his bridge. We might also find, since there was a stove, the curved poker he used to open the latch."

Without saying a word, the Count left the room, and this time those present did not feel the nervous agitation they had experienced the first time. They were convinced that Floriani was right, and no one was surprised when the Count returned and explained:

"It was the child. Everything proves it."

"You saw the shelves and the poker?"

"Yes. The nails are off the shelves and the poker is still there."

But the Countess exclaimed:

"You had better say it was his mother. Henriette is the guilty one. She must have forced her son ... "

"No," declared the knight, "the mother had nothing to do with it."

"Nonsense! They inhabited the same room. The child couldn't have done it without the mother's knowledge."

"True, they lived in the same room, but the whole thing happened in the next room, at night, while the mother was asleep."

"And the necklace?" asked the count. "It would have been found among the child's things."

"Pardon! He had gone out. The morning you found him reading, he had just come from school, and perhaps the police superintendent, instead of wasting his time with the innocent mother, would have done better to search the child's desk under his school books."

"But how do you account for the two thousand francs Henriette received each year? Are they not proof of her complicity?"

"If she had been an accomplice, would she have thanked you for the money? And was she not then closely watched? But the child, being free, could easily go to a neighboring town, bargain with some merchant, and sell him a diamond or two as he pleased, on condition that the money was sent from Paris, and this procedure could be repeated from year to year."

An indescribable uneasiness oppressed the Dreux-Soubise and her guests. There was something in Floriani's tone and attitude that had annoyed the Count from the beginning. There was a touch of irony that seemed more hostile than sympathetic. But the Count had to laugh when he said:

"This is all very imaginative and interesting, and I congratulate you on your vivid imagination."

"No, not at all," Floriani replied with the utmost seriousness, "I am not imagining anything. I am simply describing events as they must have happened."

"But what do you know about them?"

"What you told me yourself. I imagine the life of the mother and the child down there in the country; the mother's illness, the child's schemes and tricks to sell the gems to save his mother's life or at least to ease her last moments. Her illness overwhelms her. She dies. The years pass. The child becomes a man; and then - and now I will let my imagination run wild - suppose that the man feels a desire to return to the house of his childhood, that he does so, and that there he meets certain people who suspect and accuse his mother ..., can you imagine the grief and anguish of such a conversation in the house where the original drama was played out?"

His words seemed to echo for a few seconds in the silence that followed, and one could read in the faces of the Count and Countess de Dreux the confused effort to comprehend his meaning, and at the same time the anguish and anguish of such comprehension. At last the Count took the floor and said:

"Who are you, monsieur?"

"I. The knight Floriani, whom you met in Palermo and whom you have invited to your house several times."

"And what is the meaning of this story?"

"Oh! Nothing at all! It is simply a pastime as far as I am concerned. I am endeavoring to represent the pleasure that Henriette's son, if he were alive, would have in telling you that he was the culprit, and that he did it because his mother was unhappy, being about to lose the position of ... servant, on which she lived, and because the child suffered at the sight of his mother's grief."

He spoke with suppressed emotion, rose partially, and inclined toward the Countess. There could be no doubt that the knight Floriani was the son of Henriette. His bearing and his words proclaimed it. Besides, was it not his obvious intention and desire to be recognized as such?

The count hesitated. What would he do about the brazen guest? Ring the bell? Provoke a scandal? Unmask the man who had once robbed him? But that was a long time ago! And who would believe this absurd story about the guilty child? No; it was far better to accept the situation and pretend not to grasp the true meaning of the matter. So the Count turned to Floriani and exclaimed:

"Your story is very strange, very entertaining; I enjoyed it very much. But what do you think has become of this young man, this model son? I hope he has not given up the career in which he made such a brilliant debut."

"Oh! Certainly not."

"After such a debut! To steal the Queen's necklace at the age of six; the famous necklace coveted by Marie-Antoinette!"

"And to steal it," remarked Floriani, getting into the Count's mood, "without it having cost him the least trouble, without it having occurred to anyone to examine the state of the window, or to notice that the sill was too clean-that sill which he had wiped to cover the traces he had left in the thick dust. We must admit that it was enough to turn the head of a boy of that age. It was all so simple. All he had to do was desire the thing and reach out his hand for it."

"And he did reach out his hand."

"Both hands," the knight replied, laughing.

His companions got a shock. What mystery surrounded the life of the so-called Floriani? How wonderful must have been the life of this adventurer, who at six years of age was a thief, and who today, seeking excitement, or at least to satisfy a feeling of resentment, had come to defy his victim in her own house, brazen, foolish, and yet with all the grace and delicacy of a polite guest!

He rose and approached the Countess to bid her adieu. She drew back without noticing. He smiled.

"Oh! Madame, you are afraid of me! Have I gone a step too far in my role as salon magician?"

She controlled herself and answered with her usual ease:

"Not at all, monsieur. I was very interested in the legend of the dutiful son, and I am delighted to know that my necklace had such a brilliant destiny. But don't you think that the son of this woman, this Henriette, fell victim to a hereditary influence in choosing his vocation?"

He shuddered when he heard the remark, and replied:

"I am sure of it; and besides, his natural inclination to crime must have been very strong, or he would have been discouraged."

"Why so?"

"Because, as you must know, the majority of the diamonds were false. The only genuine stones were the few bought by the English jeweler; the others were sold one by one to meet the cruel necessities of life."

"It was still the queen's necklace, monsieur," the countess replied haughtily, "and that is something he, Henriette's son, did not appreciate."

"He was able to understand, madame, that the necklace, true or false, was nothing more than an object of parade, an emblem of senseless pride."

The Count made a threatening gesture, but his wife stopped him.

"Monsieur," she said, "if the man to whom you allude has even the slightest sense of honor ... "

She paused, intimidated by Floriani's cool manner.

"If that man has even the slightest sense of honor," he repeated.

She felt that she would gain nothing by speaking to him in this way, and in spite of her anger and indignation, trembling with humiliated pride, she said to him, almost politely:

"Monsieur, legend has it that when Rétaux de Villette was in possession of the Queen's necklace, he did not deface the setting. He understood that the diamonds were only the ornament, the accessory, and that the setting was the essential work, the creation of the artist, and he respected it accordingly. Do you think this man had the same feeling?"

"I have no doubt that the frame still exists. The child respected it."

"Well, monsieur, if you should happen to meet him, tell him that he is unjustly in possession of a relic which is the property and pride of a certain family, and that, although the stones have been removed, the Queen's necklace still belongs to the house of Dreux-Soubise. It belongs to us as much as our name or our honor."

The knight replied simply:

"I will tell him, Madame."

He bowed to her, saluted the count and the other guests, and departed.

Four days later, the Countess de Dreux found on the table in her chamber a red leather case bearing the Cardinal's coat of arms. She opened it and found the Queen's necklace.

But since in the life of a man who strives for unity and logic, all things must converge on the same goal - and since a little publicity never hurts - the Echo de France published these sensational lines the next day:

The Queen's necklace, the famous historical jewelry stolen from the Dreux-Soubise family, has been recovered by Arsène Lupin, who hastened to return it to its rightful owner. We cannot praise highly enough such a delicate and chivalrous act.

The Seven of Hearts

I am often asked this question, "How did you make the acquaintance of Arsène Lupin?"

My connection with Arsène Lupin was well known. The details I gather about this mysterious man, the irrefutable facts I present, the new evidence I produce, the interpretation I give to certain actions of which the public has seen only the outward manifestations without being able to discover the secret reasons or the unseen mechanism, all these establish, if not an intimacy, at least friendly relations and regular confidences.

But how did I make his acquaintance? Why was I chosen to be his historiographer? Why me, and not someone else?

The answer is simple: chance alone determined my choice; my merits were not considered. It was chance that put me in his path. It was chance that I took part in one of his strangest and most mysterious adventures; and it was chance that I was an actor in a drama of which he was the marvelous director; an obscure and intricate drama, brimming with events so exciting that I feel a certain embarrassment when I try to describe it.

The first act takes place on that memorable night of June 22, of which so much has already been said. And for my part I attribute the anomalous behavior of which I was guilty on that occasion to the unusual frame of mind in which I found myself on my return home. I had dined with some friends at the Cascade Restaurant, and all the evening, while we smoked and the orchestra played melancholy waltzes, we talked only of crimes and thefts and dark and terrible intrigues. That is always a bad overture for a night's rest.

The Saint-Martins drove away in an automobile. Jean Daspry - that delightful, carefree Daspry who died so tragically six months later on the Moroccan border - Jean Daspry and I walked back through the dark, warm night. When we arrived in front of the small house where I had lived for a year in Neuilly, on Boulevard Maillot, he said to me:

"Are you afraid?"

"What an idea!"

"But this house is so lonely ... no neighbors ... empty lots ... I'm really not a coward, and yet ... "

"Well, you're very encouraging, I must say."

"Oh! I say that as I would say anything else. The Saint-Martins impressed me with their stories of robbers and thieves."

We shook hands and said good night. I took out my key and opened the door.

"Well, that's good," I muttered, "Antoine forgot to light a candle."

Then I remembered the fact that Antoine was out of town; I had given him a short leave of absence. The darkness and silence of the night now oppressed me uncomfortably. I tiptoed up the stairs and reached my room as quickly as possible; then, contrary to my habit, I turned the key and pressed the latch.

The light of my candle gave me new courage. Nevertheless, I carefully took my revolver from its case-a large, powerful weapon-and laid it beside my bed. This precaution completed my reassurance. I lay down and, as usual, took a book from my nightstand to read myself to sleep. Then I was in for a big surprise. Instead of the paper bookmark, I found an envelope sealed with five seals of red wax. I grabbed it eagerly. It was addressed to me and labeled: Urgent.

A letter! A letter addressed to me! Who could have put it in this place? Nervously, I tore open the envelope and read:

From the moment you open this letter, whatever happens, whatever you may hear, do not move, do not utter a single cry. Otherwise you will be lost.

I am not a coward, and I can face real danger as well as anyone. But, I repeat, I was in an abnormal state of mind, my nerves strained by the events of the evening. Was there not also something startling and mysterious in my present situation, capable of disquieting the bravest mind?

My feverish fingers clutched the sheet of paper, and I read and re-read those threatening words, "Do not move, do not utter a single cry. Otherwise you will be lost."

"Nonsense!" thought I. "It's a joke; the work of a merry idiot."

I was about to laugh - a good, loud laugh. Who was stopping me? What agonizing fear was squeezing my throat?

At least I would blow out the candle. No, I couldn't do it. "Don't move or you will be lost," were the words he had written.

These autosuggestions are often more compelling than the most positive realities; but why should I fight them? All I had to do was close my eyes. I did.

At that moment, I heard a soft noise followed by crackling sounds coming from a large room that served as my library. Between the library and my sleeping quarters was a small room or anteroom.

The approach of actual danger excited me greatly, and I felt a desire to get up, seize my revolver, and hurry into the library. I did not get up; I saw one of the curtains of the left window move. There was no doubt: the curtain had moved. It was still moving. And I saw - I saw quite clearly - in the narrow space between the curtains and the window, a human figure; a bulky mass that prevented the curtains from hanging straight. And it is equally certain that the man saw me through the large meshes of the curtain. Then I understood the situation. His job was to guard me while the others carried away their prey. Should I stand up and grab my revolver? Impossible! He was there! At the slightest movement, at the slightest cry, I was lost.

Then came a terrible sound that shook the house; it was followed by two or three lighter sounds, as of a hammer striking back. At least that was the impression that formed in my confused brain. These mingled with other sounds, creating a veritable uproar that proved that the intruders were not only brazen, but also felt sure they would not be disturbed.

They were right. I did not move. Was it cowardice? No, rather weakness, the total inability to move any part of my body, combined with discretion; for why should I resist? Behind this man were ten others who would come to his aid. Should I risk my life to save a few tapestries and Bibles?

Throughout the night my torture continued. Unbearable torment, terrible torment! The noises had stopped, but I was in constant fear of their renewal. And the man! The man who guarded me, the gun in his hand. My fearful eyes remained fixed in his direction. And my heart was pounding! And from every pore of my body seeped a drop of sweat!

Suddenly I experienced a tremendous relief; a milk truck, the sound of which was familiar to me, passed on the boulevard, and at the same time I had the impression that the light of a new day was trying to steal through the closed window blinds.

At last daylight entered the room, other vehicles passed on the boulevard, and all the ghosts of the night disappeared. Then I stretched an arm out of bed, slowly and cautiously. My eyes were fixed on the curtain, searching for the exact point at which I had to shoot; I calculated exactly the movements I had to make; then, quickly, I seized my revolver and fired.

With a cry of release, I jumped up from the bed and rushed to the window. The bullet had penetrated the curtain and the window glass, but it had not touched the man - for the very good reason that there was no one there. No one! So all night long I had been hypnotized by a fold of the curtain. And during this time the malefactors had ... Furious, with an enthusiasm that nothing could have stopped, I turned the key, opened the door, crossed the anteroom, opened another door and rushed into the library. But astonishment stopped me on the threshold, gasping, amazed, even more amazed than I had been by the man's absence. All the things I assumed had been stolen, furniture, books, pictures, old tapestries, everything was in its place.

It was unbelievable. I could not believe my eyes. Regardless of this turmoil, these sounds of moving ... I made a tour, inspected the shelves, made a mental inventory of all the familiar items. Nothing was missing. And, even more disturbing, there was no sign of the intruders, no sign, no overturned chair, not a trace of a step.

"Well! Well!" I said to myself, pressing my hands on my confused head, "I'm not crazy after all! I hear something!"

Inch by inch I carefully examined the room. It was to no avail. Unless I could consider this a discovery: Under a small Persian rug I found a card - an ordinary playing card. It was the Seven of Hearts; it was like any other Seven of Hearts on French playing cards, with this small but curious exception: the outermost point of each of the seven red dots or hearts was pierced by a hole, round and regular, as if made with the point of an awl.

Nothing more. A map and a letter, found in a book. But wasn't that enough to confirm that I had not been the plaything of a dream?

Throughout the day I continued my research in the library. It was a large room, much too large for the requirements of such a house, and the decoration testified to the bizarre taste of its founder. The floor was a mosaic of multicolored stones formed into large symmetrical patterns. The walls were covered with a similar mosaic, arranged in panels, Pompeian allegories, Byzantine compositions, frescoes of the Middle Ages. A Bacchus riding a barrel. An emperor wearing a golden crown and a flowing beard, holding a sword in his right hand.

Quite high, in the manner of an artist's studio, was a large window - the only one in the room. Since this window was always open at night, it was likely that the men had entered through it with the help of a ladder. But there was no evidence of that either. The foot of the ladder would have left some marks in the soft earth under the window, but there were none. Nor were there any traces of footprints in any part of the yard.

It did not occur to me to inform the police because the facts I had before me were so absurd and contradictory. They would laugh at me. But since I was employed as a reporter by the Gil Blas at the time, I wrote a long report about my adventure, which was published in the newspaper the second day after. The article attracted some attention, but no one took it seriously. They considered it a work of fiction rather than a real-life story. The Saint-Martins sneered at me. But Daspry, who was interested in such things, came to me, investigated the matter, but came to no conclusion.

A few mornings later the doorbell rang, and Antoine came to tell me that a gentleman wished to see me. He would not give his name. I instructed Antoine to show him in. He was a man of about forty, with a very dark complexion, lively features, and whose correct, slightly frayed clothes betrayed a taste that contrasted strangely with his rather vulgar manners. Without any preamble, he said to me - in a raspy voice that confirmed my suspicions about his social standing:

"Monsieur, while sitting in a café, I picked up a copy of the Gil Blas and read your article. It interested me very much."

"Thank you."

"And here I am."

"Ah!"

"Yes, to speak with you. Are all the facts you have told me correct?"

"Absolutely correct."

"Well, in that case, I may be able to give you some information."

"Very well; go ahead."

"No, not yet. First I must be sure that the facts are exactly as you have described them."

"I have given you my word. What more proof do you want?"

"I must remain alone in this room."

"I don't understand," I said in surprise.

"It's an idea that came to me while reading your article. Certain details revealed an extraordinary correspondence with another case that had come to my attention. If I am wrong, I will say nothing more. And the only means of finding out the truth is for me to remain alone in the room."

What was behind this claim? Later, I remembered that the man was extremely nervous; but at the same time, although I was somewhat taken aback, I found nothing particularly abnormal about the man or the request he had made. Besides, my curiosity was aroused; so I replied:

"Very well. How much time do you need?"

"Oh! Three minutes - no more. I will get back to you in three minutes."

I left the room and went down the stairs. I took out my watch. One minute passed. Two minutes. Why did I feel so depressed? Why did these moments seem so pathetic and strange? Two minutes and a half ... Two minutes and three quarters. Then I heard a pistol shot.

I leaped up the stairs and entered the room. A cry of horror escaped me. In the middle of the room, the man lay on his left side, motionless. Blood flowed from a wound on his forehead. Next to his hand lay a revolver, still smoking.

But in addition to this horrible sight, my attention was drawn to another object. Two feet from the corpse, on the floor, I saw a playing card. It was the seven of hearts. I picked it up. The bottom of each of the seven points was pierced with a small round hole.

Half an hour later, the police inspector arrived, then the coroner and the head of the Sûreté, Monsieur Dudouis. I had been careful not to touch the body. The preliminary examination was very brief and revealed nothing. There were no papers in the pockets of the deceased, no name on his clothes, no initials on his linen, nothing to give any clue to his identity. The room was in the same perfect order as before. The furniture had not been touched. But this man had not come to my house merely to kill himself, or because he considered my place the most suitable for his suicide! There must have been a motive for his desperate act, and that motive was undoubtedly the result of a new fact which he established during the three minutes he was alone.

What was this fact? What had he seen? What terrible secret had been revealed to him? There was no answer to these questions. But at the last moment an incident occurred which seemed to us to be of considerable importance. As two policemen lifted the body to place it on a stretcher, moving the left hand, a crumpled card fell from it. The card bore these words, "Georges Andermatt, 37 Rue de Berry."

What did that mean? Georges Andermatt was a wealthy banker in Paris, the founder and president of the Metal Exchange, which had given a massive boost to the metal industry in France. He lived in princely style, owning numerous automobiles, carriages and an expensive racing stable. His social circumstances were very exquisite, and Madame Andermatt was known for her grace and beauty.

"Can that be the man's name?" asked I.

The chief of the Sûreté bent over him.

"It isn't. Monsieur Andermatt is a thin man, and somewhat gray."

"But why this card?"

"Do you have a telephone, monsieur?"

"Yes, in the vestibule. Come with me."

He looked in the phone book, then asked for the number 41521.

"Is Monsieur Andermatt at home? ... Please tell him that Monsieur Dudouis asks him to come immediately to 102 Boulevard Maillot. It is very important."

Twenty minutes later, Monsieur Andermatt arrived in his automobile. After the circumstances were explained to him, he was ushered in to see the body. He showed considerable emotion and spoke softly and apparently unwillingly:

"Etienne Varin," he said.

"Do you know him?"

"No ... or, at least, yes ... only by sight. His brother ..."

"Ah! He has a brother?"

"Yes, Alfred Varin. He came to me once on a business matter ... I have forgotten what it was."

"Where does he live?"

"The two brothers live together ... Rue de Provence, I think."

"Do you know of any reason why he would commit suicide?"

"None."

"He was holding a card in his hand. It was your card with your address."

"I don't understand that. It must have been there by chance, as the investigation will reveal."

A very strange coincidence, I thought, and I felt that the others had the same impression.

I found the same impression the next day in the newspapers and among all my friends with whom I discussed the affair. In the midst of the mysteries that surrounded it, after the double discovery of the Seven of Hearts with seven holes, after the two obscure events that had taken place in my house, this business card promised to shed some light on the affair. Through it, the truth might be revealed. But contrary to expectations, Monsieur Andermatt did not provide any explanation. He said:

"I have told you all I know. What more can I do? I am very surprised that my card was found in such a place, and I sincerely hope that the matter will be cleared up."

It didn't. The official investigation revealed that the Varin brothers were from Switzerland, led an erratic life under various names, frequented gambling dens, and associated with a gang of foreigners linked by police to a series of robberies in which their involvement was proven. At 24 rue de Provence, where the Varin brothers had lived six years earlier, no one knew what had become of them.

I confess that the case seemed so complicated and puzzling to me that I did not believe the problem would ever be solved, and so I decided not to waste any more time on it. But Jean Daspry, whom I met frequently at that time, became more interested in it every day. It was he who pointed out to me that article from a foreign newspaper which was picked up and commented on by the entire press. It read as follows:

The first trial of a new model of submarine, intended to revolutionize naval warfare, will take place in the presence of the former Emperor at a place kept secret until the last minute. Through an indiscretion, its name has been revealed; it is 'Seven of Hearts'.

The Seven of Hearts! This posed a new problem. Could there be a connection between the name of the submarine and the events we recounted? But what was the nature of the connection? What happened here could have nothing to do with the submarine.

"What do you know about it?" said Daspry to me. "The most diverse effects often come from the same cause."

The next day, the following news story was published:

It was said that the plans of the new submarine 'Seven of Hearts' had been drawn up by French engineers, who, after vainly seeking the support of their countrymen, subsequently entered into negotiations with the British Admiralty.

I do not wish to give undue publicity to certain delicate matters which once caused considerable excitement. But now that all danger of injury from this has passed, I must speak of the article which appeared in the Echo de France, which caused such a sensation at the time, and which threw considerable light on the mystery of the Seven of Hearts. This is the article as it was published with Salvator's signature:

THE AFFAIR OF THE SEVEN OF HEARTS. VEIL LIFTED.

We will be brief. Ten years ago, a young mining engineer, Louis Lacombe, wishing to devote his time and fortune to certain studies, resigned his then position and rented a small house at number 102 Boulevard Maillot, recently built and furnished for an Italian count. Through the agency of the Varin brothers of Lausanne, one of whom helped with the preliminary experiments and the other acted as financial agent, the young engineer was introduced to Georges Andermatt, founder of the Metal Exchange.

After several conversations, he succeeded in interesting the banker in a submarine on which he was working, and it was agreed that as soon as the invention was perfected, Monsieur Andermatt would use his influence with the Minister of the Navy to obtain a series of trials under the direction of the government. For two years Louis Lacombe was a frequent visitor at Andermatt's house, presenting to the banker the various improvements he had made to his original plans, until one day, when he was satisfied with the perfection of his work, he asked Monsieur Andermatt to speak to the Minister of the Navy. That day Louis Lacombe dined at Monsieur Andermatt's house. He left the house at about half past eleven at night. He has not been seen since.

A glance at the newspapers of the time shows that the young man's family made all sorts of inquiries, but without success; and it was the general opinion that Louis Lacombe - who was known as an original and visionary young man - had quietly departed for parts unknown.

Let us accept this theory - improbable as it may be - and consider another question of great importance to our country: what happened to the plans of the submarine? Did Louis Lacombe get rid of them? Have they been destroyed?

After a thorough investigation, we can state with certainty that the plans exist and are now in the possession of the two Varin brothers. How did they come into this possession? That is a question that has not yet been resolved; nor do we know why they did not try to sell them earlier. Did they fear that their ownership of them would be challenged? If so, they have lost that fear, and we can definitely announce that the plans of Louis Lacombe are now the property of a foreign power, and we are able to publish the correspondence that existed between the Varin brothers and the representative of that foreign power. The 'Seven of Hearts' invented by Louis Lacombe has actually been constructed by our neighbor.

Will the invention fulfill the optimistic expectations of those who participated in this treacherous act?

And a postscript adds:

Later ... Our special correspondent informs us that the first test of the 'Seven of Hearts' has not been satisfactory. It is very likely that the plans sold and delivered by the Varin brothers did not include the final document that Louis Lacombe took with him on the day of the meeting with Monsieur Andermatt and on the day of his disappearance, a document that was essential for a thorough understanding of the invention. It contained a summary of the inventor's final conclusions, as well as estimates and figures not included in the other papers. Without this document, the plans are incomplete; on the other hand, without the plans, the document is worthless.

Now is the time to act and take back what is ours. It may be a difficult matter, but we are relying on Mr. Andermatt's help. It will be in his interest to explain his hitherto so strange and inscrutable behavior. He will explain not only why he concealed these facts at the time of Etienne Varin's suicide, but also why he never revealed the disappearance of the paper - a fact of which he was well aware. He will tell why he paid spies to watch the Varin brothers' movements for the last six years. We expect from him not only words, but actions. And we want it now. Otherwise ...

The threat was clearly stated. But what did it consist of? What whip was Salvator, the anonymous author of the article, holding over Monsieur Andermatt's head?

An army of reporters pounced on the banker, and ten interviewers announced how contemptuously they had been treated. The Echo de France then announced its position in these words:

Whether Monsieur Andermatt is willing or not, he will be our collaborator from now on, in the work we have begun.

Daspry and I were having dinner together the day this announcement appeared. That evening, while the papers were spread out on my table, we discussed the matter and examined it from all sides with that despair which a man feels when he walks in the dark and stumbles over the same obstacles again and again. Suddenly, without any warning, the door opened and a lady entered. Her face was hidden behind a thick veil. I rose at once and went up to her.

"Is it you, monsieur, who lives here?" she asked.

"Yes, madame, but I do not understand ... "

"The gate was not locked," she explained.

"But the door to the vestibule?"

She didn't answer, and it occurred to me that she had used the service entrance. How did she know the way? Then there was a silence that was quite awkward. She looked at Daspry, and I was forced to introduce him. I asked her to sit down and explain the reason for her visit. She lifted her veil, and I saw that she was a brunette, with even features, and although she was not beautiful, she was attractive - especially because of her sad, dark eyes.

"I am Madame Andermatt," she said.

"Madame Andermatt!" I repeated with astonishment.

After a brief pause, she continued in a voice and manner that seemed quite easy and natural:

"I came to see you about this matter - you know. I thought I might be able to get some information ..."

"My God, Madame, I know nothing except what has already appeared in the newspapers. But if you would tell me how I can help you ..."

"I don't know ... I don't know."

Only then did I suspect that her calm demeanor was only an act, and that beneath that calmness lay a deep sorrow. For a moment we were silent and embarrassed. Then Daspry stepped forward and said:

"Will you permit me to ask you a few questions?"

"Yes, yes," she cried, "I will answer."

"You will answer ... whatever those questions may be?"

"Yes."

"Did you know Louis Lacombe?" he asked.

"Yes, through my husband."

"When did you last see him?"

"The night he had dinner with us."

"Was there anything then that made you think you would never see him again?"

"No. But he had talked about a trip to Russia ... in a vague way."

"Then you expected to see him again?"

"Yes. He was to have dinner with us two days later."

"How do you explain his disappearance?"

"I can't explain it."

"And Mr. Andermatt?"

"I don't know."

"But the article in the Echo de France shows ..."

"Yes, that the Varin brothers had something to do with his disappearance."

"Is that your opinion?"

"Yes."

"On what do you base your opinion?"

"When he left our house, Louis Lacombe was carrying a bag containing all the papers relating to his invention. Two days later, in a conversation with one of the Varin brothers, my husband learned that the papers were in their possession."

"And he did not denounce them?"

"No."

"Why not?"

"Because there was something else in the bag besides the papers of Louis Lacombe."

"What was it?"

She hesitated, was about to say something, but finally fell silent. Daspry continued:

"I suppose that is why your husband kept a close watch on their movements instead of informing the police. He hoped to recover the papers and, at the same time, that compromising article that allowed the two brothers to ply him with threats and blackmail."

"About him, and about me."

"Ah! About you, too?"

"About me, in particular."

She uttered the last words in a hollow voice. Daspry watched her; he walked back and forth for a moment, then turned to her and asked:

"Have you written to Louis Lacombe?"

"Of course. My husband had business with him ... "

"Apart from these business letters, have you written to Louis Lacombe ... other letters? Forgive my persistence, but I really need to know the truth. Have you written any other letters?"

"Yes," she answered, blushing.

"And these letters came into the possession of the Varin brothers?"

"Yes."

"Does Monsieur Andermatt know about them?"

"He has not seen them, but Alfred Varin told him of their existence and threatened to publish them if my husband did anything against him. My husband was afraid ... it was a scandal."

"But he tried to get the letters back?"

"I think so; but I don't know. You see, after the last conversation with Alfred Varin, and after some harsh words between me and my husband, in which he called me to account, we live like strangers."

"In that case, since you have nothing to lose, what do you fear?"

"I may be indifferent to him now, but I am the woman he loved, the woman he would still love-oh! I am quite sure of it," she murmured in a fervent voice, "he would still love me if he had not come into possession of those accursed letters ... "

"What, has he succeeded? ... But the two brothers still resisted him?"

"Yes, and they boasted of having a safe hiding place."

"And?"

"I think my husband discovered that hiding place."

"Ah! Where was it?"

"Here."

"Here!" I exclaimed, startled.

"Yes. I have always had that suspicion. Louis Lacombe was very inventive, and amused himself in his leisure hours by building safes and locks. No doubt the Varin brothers were aware of this fact and used one of Lacombe's safes, in which they may have hidden the letters ... and other things."

"But they didn't live here," I said.

"Before you came, four months ago, the house had been empty for some time. And they may have thought that your presence here wouldn't bother them when they came for the papers. But they did not reckon with my husband, who came here on the night of June 22, broke open the safe, took what was wanted and left his card to tell the two brothers that he no longer feared them and that their positions were now reversed. Two days later, after reading the article in the Gil Blas, Etienne Varin came here, stayed alone in this room, found the safe empty, and ... killed himself."

After a moment, Daspry said:

"A very simple theory ... Has Monsieur Andermatt spoken to you since then?"

"No."

"Has his attitude toward you changed in any way? Does he seem more somber, more anxious?"

"No, I have not noticed any change."

"And yet you think he has secured the letters. In my opinion, he doesn't have the letters, and it wasn't him who came here on the night of June 22."

"Then who was it?"

"The mysterious individual who is in charge of this affair, who holds all the strings and whose invisible but far-reaching power we have felt from the beginning. It was he who entered this house with his friends on June 22; it was he who discovered the hiding place of the papers; it was he who deposited Monsieur Andermatt's card; it is he who now possesses the correspondence and the evidence of the Varin brothers' treachery."

"Who is he?" asked I impatiently.

"The man who writes the letters to the Echo de France .... Salvator. Don't we have convincing evidence of that fact? Does he not mention in his letters certain details which no one can know except the man who thus discovered the secrets of the two brothers?"

"Well then," stammered Madame Andermatt in great anxiety, "he has my letters too, and it is he who is now threatening my husband. My God! What am I to do?"

"Write to him," Daspry declared. "Confide in him without reservation. Tell him everything you know and everything you will learn in the future. Your interest and his interest are the same. He is not working against Monsieur Andermatt, but against Alfred Varin. Help him."

"How?"

"Does your husband have the document that completes Louis Lacombe's plans?"

"Yes."

"Tell that to Salvator, and if possible, get him the document. Write to him at once. You risk nothing."

The advice was bold, even dangerous at first glance, but Madame Andermatt had no choice. Besides, as Daspry had said, she was taking no chances. If the unknown writer were an enemy, this step would not aggravate the situation. If he were a stranger seeking to achieve a specific purpose, he would attach only secondary importance to these letters. Whatever might happen, it was the only solution that presented itself to her, and she, in her anxiety, was only too willing to act on it. She thanked us profusely and promised to keep us informed.

In fact, two days later she sent us the following letter she had received from Salvator:

"Haven't found the letters, but I will get them. Stay calm. I am watching everything. S."

I looked at the letter. It was written in the same handwriting as the note I had found in my book on the night of June 22.

Daspry was right. Salvator was indeed the author of this affair.

We began to see a little light coming out of the darkness surrounding us, and an unexpected light was shed on certain points; but other points still remained in the dark - for example, the finding of the two Seven of Hearts. Perhaps I was unnecessarily troubled by these two cards, whose seven pierced points had appeared to me under such perplexing circumstances! Still, I couldn't help but wonder: what role will they play in the drama? What significance will they have? What conclusion must be drawn from the fact that the submarine constructed according to the plans of Louis Lacombe bore the name "Seven of Hearts"?

Daspry cared little for the other two maps; he devoted all his attention to another problem which he considered more urgent; he was looking for the famous hiding place.

"And who knows," he said, "I may find the letters that Salvator did not - perhaps by accident. It is unlikely that the Varin brothers would have removed the weapon, so valuable to them, from a place they thought inaccessible."

And he kept searching. After a short time, the large room held no more secrets for him, so he expanded his investigation to the other rooms. He examined the interior and the exterior, the stones of the foundation, the tiles in the walls; he lifted the slates of the roof.

One day he came with a pickaxe and a spade, gave me the spade, kept the pickaxe, pointed to the adjacent vacant lots and said, "Come."

I followed him, but I lacked his enthusiasm. He divided the undeveloped land into several sections, which he examined in turn. At last, in a corner, in the angle formed by the walls of two neighboring owners, a small pile of earth and gravel, covered with thorns and grass, attracted his attention. He attacked it. I was forced to help him. For an hour we struggled unsuccessfully under the hot sun. I was discouraged, but Daspry spurred me on. His zeal was as strong as ever.

At last Daspry's pickaxe unearthed some bones - the remains of a skeleton with some scraps of clothing still hanging on. Suddenly I turned pale. I had discovered a small piece of iron in the earth, shaped like a rectangle, on which I thought I saw red stains. I bent down and picked it up. The small iron plate was exactly the size of a playing card, and the red spots, made with red lead, were arranged on it in a manner resembling the seven of hearts, and each spot was pierced with a round hole resembling the perforations in the two playing cards.

"Listen, Daspry, I've had enough of this. You can stay if you're interested. But I'm leaving now."

Was that just the expression of my agitated nerves? Or was it the result of an arduous task, carried out under a burning sun? I know that I trembled when I left, and that I went to bed, where I remained for forty-eight hours, restless and feverish, haunted by skeletons that danced around me and threw their bleeding hearts at my head.

Daspry was faithful to me. He came to my house every day and stayed three or four hours, which he spent in the big room, rummaging, knocking, searching.

"The letters are here, in this room," he would say from time to time, "they are here. I'll bet my life on it."

On the morning of the third day I got up - still feeble, but cured. A hearty breakfast cheered me up. But a letter I received that afternoon contributed more than anything else to my complete recovery and aroused in me a lively curiosity. This was the letter:

Monsieur,

The drama, the first act of which occurred on the night of June 22, is now drawing to a close. Circumstances compel me to bring the two principal actors of this drama face to face, and I wish this meeting to take place at your house, if you will be kind enough to place it at my disposal for this evening from nine to eleven o'clock. It will be advisable to release your servant for the evening, and perhaps you will be kind enough to give the field to the two antagonists. You will remember that when I visited your house on the night of June 22, I took excellent care of your property. I think I would do you an injustice if I doubted for a moment your absolute discretion in this matter. Yours faithfully,

SALVATOR

I was amused by the jocular tone of his letter and also by the whimsical nature of his request. There was a charming display of confidence and candor in his language, and nothing in the world could have induced me to deceive him, or to repay his confidence with ingratitude.

I gave my servant a theater ticket, and he left the house at eight o'clock. A few minutes later Daspry came. I showed him the letter.

"Well?" he said.

"Well, I have left the garden gate unlocked so that anyone can enter."

"And you ... are you going away?"

"Not at all. I intend to stay here."

"But he asks you to leave ... "

"But I'm not going to leave. I'll be discreet, but I'm determined to see what happens."

"My goodness!" exclaimed Daspry, laughing, "you are right, and I will stay with you. I don't want to miss it."

We were interrupted by the sound of the doorbell.

"Already there?" said Daspry, "twenty minutes ahead of time! Unbelievable!"

I went to the door and ushered the visitor in. It was Madame Andermatt. She was weak and nervous, and in a stammering voice she said:

"My husband ... is coming ... he has an appointment ... they want to give him the letters ... "

"How do you know that?", I asked.

"By chance. A message came for my husband while we were at dinner. The servant gave it to me by mistake. My husband quickly took it, but he was too late. I had read it."

"You read it?"

"Yes. It read something like this: `Be at Boulevard Maillot tonight at nine o'clock with the papers relating to the affair. In exchange, the letters.' So I hurried here after dinner."

"Unknown to your husband?"

"Yes."

"What do you think about that?" asked Daspry, turning to me.

"I think, as you do, that Monsieur Andermatt is one of the invited guests."

"Yes, but for what purpose?"

"We will find out in a moment."

I led the men into a large room. Three of us could comfortably hide behind the velvet fireplace mantle and observe everything that was to happen in the room. We sat down there, with Madame Andermatt in the middle.

The clock struck nine. A few minutes later the garden gate creaked on its hinges. I confess that I was very excited. I was about to learn the key to the mystery. The terrifying events of the last few weeks were about to be explained, and the final battle was to be fought before my eyes. Daspry seized Madame Andermatt's hand and said to her:

"Not a word, not a movement! Whatever you may see or hear, be silent!"

Someone entered. It was Alfred Varin. I recognized him immediately because he looked very much like his brother Etienne. He had the same limping gait, the same corpse-pale face with the black beard.

He entered with the nervous expression of a man accustomed to fear the presence of traps and ambushes, who scents and avoids them. He looked around the room, and I had the impression that he did not like the fireplace covered with a velvet portiere. He took three steps in our direction when something caused him to turn and walk toward the old mosaic king with the flowing beard and flaming sword, whom he examined closely, sitting down on a chair and tracing with his fingers the outline of the shoulders and head and feeling certain parts of the face. Suddenly he jumped up from the chair and walked away from it. He had heard the sound of approaching footsteps. Monsieur Andermatt appeared at the door.

"You! You!" the banker exclaimed. "Was it you who brought me here?"

"I? Not at all," Varin protested in a rough, jerky voice that reminded me of his brother, "on the contrary, it was your letter that brought me here."

"My letter?"

"A letter signed by you, in which you offered me ... "

"I never wrote to you," Monsieur Andermatt declared.

"You didn't write to me!?"

Instinctively Varin was on guard, not against the banker, but against the unknown enemy who had lured him into this trap. A second time he glanced in our direction, then headed for the door. But Monsieur Andermatt blocked his way.

"Well, where are you going, Varin?"

"There's something about this affair I don't like. I'm going home. Good evening."

"Just a moment!"

"There's no need for that, Mr. Andermatt. I have nothing to say to you."

"But I have something to tell you, and this is a good time to do it."

"Let me pass."

"No, you will not pass."

Varin backed away from the banker's determined stance as he muttered:

"Well, hurry up then."

One thing puzzled me, and I have no doubt that my two companions felt a similar sensation. Why was Salvator not there? Was he not a necessary participant in this conference? Or was he content to let the two adversaries fight it all out among themselves? In any case, his absence was a great disappointment, although it did not detract from the drama of the situation.

After a moment, Monsieur Andermatt approached Varin and said, face to face, eye to eye:

"Now, after all these years and when you have nothing more to fear, you can answer me frankly: What have you done with Louis Lacombe?"

"What a question! As if I knew anything about him!"

"Yes, you do know! You and your brother were his constant companions, almost lived with him in this house. You knew all about his plans and his work. And the last night I saw Louis Lacombe, when I said good-bye to him at my door, I saw two men slinking away in the shade of the trees. That's what I'm willing to swear to."

"Well, what has that to do with me?"

"The two men were you and your brother."

"Prove it."

"The best proof is that two days later you yourself showed me the papers and plans that belonged to Lacombe and offered to sell them. How did these papers come into your possession?"

"I have already told you, Monsieur Andermatt, that we found them on his table the morning after Lacombe's disappearance."

"That is a lie!"

"Prove it."

"The law will prove it."

"Then why didn't you go to court?"

"Why? Ah! Why ... " the banker stammered emotionally.

"You know very well, Monsieur Andermatt, that if you had had the slightest certainty of our guilt, our little threat would not have stopped you."

"What threat? Those letters? Do you think I ever gave a thought to those letters?"

"If you didn't care about the letters, why did you offer me thousands of francs for their return? And why did you have my brother and me pursued like wild animals?"

"To get the plans back."

"Bullshit! You wanted the letters. You knew that once you were in possession of the letters you could betray us. Oh! No, I couldn't part with them!"

He laughed heartily, but stopped suddenly and said:

"But, enough of that! We are only moving on old ground. We're not making any progress. We should leave things as they are."

"We will not leave things as they are," said the banker, "and since you have referred to the letters, let me tell you that you will not leave this house until you have delivered those letters."

"I will leave when I please."

"You will not."

"Be careful, Mr. Andermatt. I warn you ... "

"I say you won't go."

"We'll see about that," Varin shouted so angrily that Madame Andermatt could not suppress a cry of fear. Varin must have heard him, for he was now trying to make his way out. M. Andermatt pushed him back. Then I saw him put his hand in his coat pocket.

"For the last time, let me pass," he shouted.

"The letters, first!"

Varin drew a revolver and pointed it at Monsieur Andermatt, saying:

"Yes or no?"

The banker stooped quickly. Then a pistol shot rang out. The gun fell out of Varin's hand. I was astonished.

The shot was fired near me. It was Daspry who had fired it at Varin, so that he dropped the revolver. The next moment Daspry stood between the two men and looked at Varin; he said to him with a mocking smile:

"You were lucky, my friend, very lucky. I shot at your hand and only hit the revolver."

Both looked at him in amazement. Then he turned to the banker and said:

"I beg your pardon, monsieur, for interfering in your affairs; but you are really playing a very bad game. Let me hold the cards."

Turning again to Varin, Daspry said:

"This is between you and me, comrade, and play fair. Hearts is trump, and I play sevens."

Then Daspry held up the little iron plate before Varin's stunned eyes, marked with the seven red dots. It was a terrible shock to Varin. Pale-faced, staring, and with an air of intense agony, the man seemed mesmerized at the sight of her.

"Who are you?" he gasped.

"One who meddles in other people's affairs, all the way down."

"What do you want?"

"What you brought here tonight."

"I didn't bring anything."

"Yes, you did, or you wouldn't have come. This morning you received an invitation to come here at nine o'clock and bring all the papers you have. You are here. Where are the papers?"

There was a tone of authority in Daspry's voice and manner that I did not understand; his manner was otherwise quite mild and conciliatory. Completely overwhelmed, Varin put his hand on one of his pockets and said:

"The papers are here."

"All of them?"

"Yes."

"All the ones you took from Louis Lacombe and then sold to Major von Lieben?"

"Yes."

"Are these the copies or the originals?"

"I have the originals."

"How much do you want for them?"

"One hundred thousand francs."

"You're crazy," Daspry said. "After all, the major only gave you twenty thousand, and that was like money thrown into the sea, since the boat was a failure in the preliminary tests."

"You didn't understand the plans."

"The plans are not complete."

"Then why are you asking me for them?"

"Because I want them. I offer you five thousand francs-not a sou more."

"Ten thousand. Not one sou less."

"Agreed," said Daspry, who now turned to Monsieur Andermatt and said:

"Monsieur will kindly sign a check for the amount."

"But ... I don't have ... "

"Your checkbook? Here it is."

Astonished, Monsieur Andermatt examined the checkbook Daspry handed him.

"It's mine," he gasped. "How can that be?"

"No idle talk, monsieur, if you will. All you have to do is sign it."

The banker took out his fountain pen, filled out the check, and signed it. Varin held out his hand to him.

"Put your hand down," Daspry said, "there's one more thing." Then he said to the banker, "You wanted some letters, didn't you?"

"Yes, a package of letters."

"Where are they, Varin?"

"I didn't get them."

"Where are they, Varin?"

"I don't know. My brother had them in his hand."

"They are hidden in this room."

"If they are, you know where they are."

"How should I know?"

"Wasn't it you who found the hiding place? You seem to be as well informed as Salvator."

"The letters are not in the hiding place."

"Yes, they are."

"Open them."

Varin looked at him challengingly. Were not Daspry and Salvator one and the same person? Everything pointed to that conclusion. If so, Varin risked nothing by revealing an already known hiding place.

"Open it," Daspry repeated.

"I don't have the Seven of Hearts."

"Yes, here it is," Daspry said, handing him the iron plate. Varin jerked back, startled, and called out:

"No, no, I don't want it."

"Never mind," Daspry replied, walking up to the bearded king, climbing onto a chair and placing the heart sieve on the lower part of the sword so that the edges of the iron plate exactly matched the two edges of the sword. Then, using an awl, which he inserted into each of the seven holes in turn, he pressed on seven of the tesserae. When he pressed on the seventh, a clicking sound rang out, and the entire bust of the king turned on a pivot, revealing a large steel-lined opening. It really was a fireproof safe.

"You see, Varin, the safe is empty."

"I see that. Then my brother took out the letters."

Daspry got down from the chair, walked up to Varin and said:

"So, no more nonsense with me. There is another hiding place. Where is it?"

"There isn't."

"Do you want money? How much?"

"Ten thousand."

"Monsieur Andermatt, are these letters worth ten thousand francs to you?"

"Yes," said the banker in a firm voice.

Varin closed the safe, took the seven of hearts, and put them back on the sword, in the same place. He stabbed the awl into each of the seven holes. There was the same clicking sound, but this time, oddly enough, it was only one part of the safe spinning on its axis, revealing a rather small safe built into the door of the larger one. The parcel with the letters was here, tied with a ribbon and sealed. Varin handed the packet to Daspry. The latter turned to the banker and asked:

"Is the check ready, Monsieur Andermatt?"

"Yes."

"And you also have the last document you received from Louis Lacombe - the one in which the plans of the submarine are completed?"

"Yes."

The exchange was complete. Daspry pocketed the document and the checks and offered the package of letters to Monsieur Andermatt.

"This is what you wanted, monsieur."

The banker hesitated for a moment, as if afraid to touch the cursed letters he had so eagerly sought. Then, with a nervous movement, he took them. Near me I heard a groan. I grasped Madame Andermatt's hand. It was cold.

"I believe, monsieur," Daspry said to the banker, "that our business is finished. It was only by mere chance that I was able to do you a good turn. Good night."

Monsieur Andermatt withdrew. He had in his bag the letters his wife had written to Louis Lacombe.

"Wonderful!" exclaimed Daspry, delighted. "Everything is coming our way. Now we have only to conclude our little affair, comrade. Have you got the papers?"

"Here they are, all of them."

Daspry examined them carefully and then put them in his pocket.

"That's right. You kept your word," he said.

"But ... "

"But what?"

"The two checks? The money?" said Varin eagerly.

"Well, you have a lot of confidence, my man. How dare you ask for such a thing?"

"I only demand what is due me."

"Can you demand wages for the return of papers you have stolen? Well, I think not!"

Varin was beside himself. He was trembling with rage; his eyes were bloodshot.

"The money ... the twenty thousand ..." he stammered.

"Impossible! I need it myself."

"The money!"

"Come on, be reasonable, and don't get upset. It won't do any good."

Daspry grabbed his arm so violently that Varin let out a cry of pain. Daspry continued:

"Now you can go. The air will do you good. Perhaps you will want me to show you the way. Ah! yes, we will go together to the empty lot nearby, and I will show you a small mound of earth and stones, and under it ... "

"This is wrong! That is false!"

"Oh! no, it is true. The little iron plate with the seven dots on it came from there. Louis Lacombe always carried it with him, and you buried it with the body-and with some other things that will prove very interesting to a judge and jury."

Varin covered his face with his hands and muttered:

"All right, I'm beat. Don't say any more. But there's one question I'd like to ask you. I would like to know ... "

"What is it?"

"Was there a small casket in the big safe?"

"Yes."

"Was it there on the night of June 22?"

"Yes."

"What did it contain?"

"Everything the Varin brothers had put in it.... A pretty collection of diamonds and pearls that said brothers had collected here and there."

"And did you take it?"

"Of course I did. Can you blame me?"

"I understand ... that it was the disappearance of that casket that made my brother kill himself."

"Probably. The disappearance of your correspondence was not a sufficient motive. But the disappearance of the casket ... is that all you want to ask me?"

"One more thing: your name?"

"You ask that with the intention of revenge."

"God knows! The tables can be turned. Today you're on top. Tomorrow ..."

"You will be."

"I hope so. Your name?"

"Arsène Lupin."

"Arsène Lupin!"

The man staggered as if a heavy blow had stunned him. Those two words had taken all hope from him.

Daspry laughed and said:

"Ah! Did you think that a Monsieur Durand or Dupont could settle such a matter? No, it required the skill and cunning of Arsène Lupin. And now that you know my name, go and prepare your revenge. Arsène Lupin will be waiting for you."

Then he pushed the stunned Varin through the door.

"Daspry! Daspry!" I shouted, pushing aside the curtain. He ran to me.

"What, what's the matter?"

"Madame Andermatt is ill."

He hurried to her, made her inhale some salts, and, while attending to her, questioned me:

"Well, what was it?"

"The letters from Louis Lacombe that you gave to her husband."

He slapped his forehead and said:

"Did she think I could do such a thing! ... But of course she would. Fool that I am!"

Madame Andermatt had now regained consciousness. Daspry took from his pocket a small parcel exactly like the one Monsieur Andermatt had carried away.

"Here are your letters, madame. These are the real letters."

"But ... the others?"

"The others are the same, rewritten by me and carefully worded. Your husband will find nothing objectionable in them, and will not suspect the exchange, since they were taken from the safe in his presence."

"But the handwriting ... "

"There is no handwriting that cannot be imitated."

She thanked me with the same words she would have used to a man of her acquaintance, from which I concluded that she had not witnessed the final scene between Varin and Arsène Lupin. But this surprising revelation embarrassed me. Lupin! My comrade was none other than Arsène Lupin. I could not understand it. But he said, offhandedly:

"You can say goodbye to Jean Daspry."

"Ah!"

"Yes, Jean Daspry is going on a long trip. I will send him to Morocco. There he may find a death worthy of him. I may say that is his expectation."

"But Arsène Lupin will stay?"

"Oh! Most certainly. Arsène Lupin is on the threshold of his career and he expects ..."

Curiosity forced me to interrupt him. I led him away from Madame Andermatt and asked:

"Did you discover the smaller safe yourself, where the letters were?"

"Yes, after much trouble. I found it yesterday afternoon while you were asleep. And yet, God knows, it was simple enough! But the simplest things are those that usually escape us." Then he showed me the Seven of Hearts and added, "Of course, I guessed that this card must be placed on the sword of the Mosaic King to open the larger vault."

"How did you guess that?"

"Quite simply. Through private information, I knew this fact when I came here on the evening of June 22 ..."

"After you left me ... "

"Yes, after I had turned the subject of our conversation to stories of crime and robbery, which would surely put you in such a nervous state that you would not leave your bed, but would allow me to finish my search undisturbed."

"The plan worked perfectly."

"Well, I knew when I got here that there was a casket hidden in a safe with a secret lock, and that the Seven of Hearts was the key to that lock.

All I had to do was put the card in the place that was obviously intended for it. An hour's investigation showed me where the spot was."

"An hour!"

"Look at the guy in the mosaic."

"The old emperor?"

"The old emperor is an exact representation of the King of Hearts on all the playing cards."

"That's right. But how can the Seven of Hearts open the larger vault once and the smaller vault once? And why did you only open the larger safe to begin with? I mean on the night of June 22."

"Because I always placed the Seven of Hearts the same way. I never changed the position. But yesterday I observed that by turning the card over, by turning it upside down, the arrangement of the seven dots on the mosaic was changed."

"Truly!"

"Of course! But a person must think of such things."

"There is something else: you did not know the history of these letters until Madame Andermatt ... "

"Spoke of them before me? No. For I found nothing in the safe but the correspondence of the two brothers, which revealed their betrayal of the plans, except the casket."

"Then it was coincidence that you first researched the history of the two brothers and then looked for the plans and documents of the submarine?"

"Simply coincidence."

"For what purpose did you conduct the search?"

"My God!" exclaimed Daspry with a laugh, "how interested you are in the subject!"

"The subject fascinates me."

"Very well, after I have escorted Madame Andermatt to a carriage and sent a short story to the Echo de France, I will return and tell you all about it."

He sat down and wrote one of those short, clear articles that served to amuse and amaze the public. Who doesn't remember the sensation that this article caused all over the world?

Arsène Lupin solved the problem recently presented by Salvator. Having come into possession of all the documents and original plans of the engineer Louis Lacombe, he put them at the disposal of the Minister of the Navy and headed a subscription list to present to the nation the first submarine constructed according to these plans. His subscription is twenty thousand francs.

"Twenty thousand francs! Mon. Andermatt's checks?" I exclaimed as he handed me the paper to read.

"Exactly. It was quite right for Varin to cash his treason."

And so I made the acquaintance of Arsène Lupin. So I learned that Jean Daspry, a member of my club, was none other than Arsène Lupin, the gentleman thief. Thus was born a very pleasant friendship with this famous man, and thanks to the confidence with which he graced me, I became his very humble and faithful historiographer.

The safe of Madame Imbert

At three o'clock in the morning there were still half a dozen carriages in front of one of those little houses which form only the side of the Boulevard Berthier. The door of this house opened, and a number of guests, male and female, stepped out. Most of them got into their carriages and were quickly driven away, leaving only two men who went down Courcelles, where they parted, since one of them lived on that street. The other decided to return on foot as far as the Porte-Maillot. It was a beautiful winter night, clear and cold; a night when a brisk walk is pleasant and refreshing.

But after a few minutes he had the unpleasant impression that he was being followed. Turning around, he saw a man prowling among the trees. He was not a coward; nevertheless, he thought it advisable to increase his pace. Then his pursuer began to run, and he thought it wise to draw his revolver and face him. But he had no time. The man rushed at him and attacked him fiercely. Immediately they were engaged in a desperate struggle in which he felt that his unknown assailant had the advantage. He cried out for help, fought back, and was thrown onto a pile of gravel, grabbed by the throat, and gagged with a handkerchief that his attacker forced into his mouth. His eyes fell shut and the man, crushing him with his weight, rose to defend himself against an unexpected attack. A blow from the cane and a kick from the boot; the man uttered two cries of pain and fled, limping and cursing. Without pursuing the fugitive, the newcomer bent over the man lying on the ground and inquired:

"Are you hurt, sir?"

He was not hurt, but he was dazed and unable to get up. His rescuer procured a carriage, put him in it, and accompanied him to his home on the Avenue de la Grande-Armée. Once there, somewhat recovered, he showered his rescuer with thanks.

"I owe my life to you, monsieur, and I will not forget it. I don't want to worry my wife at this hour, but tomorrow she will be happy to thank you personally. Come and have breakfast with us. My name is Ludovic Imbert. May I ask you about yours?"

"Certainly, Monsieur."

And he handed Monsieur Imbert a card with the name: Arsène Lupin.

At that time, Arsène Lupin did not yet enjoy the fame that the Cahorn affair, his escape from the Prison de la Santé, and other brilliant deeds later brought him. He had not even used the name Arsène Lupin. The name had been specially invented to designate the savior of Monsieur Imbert; that is, it was in this affair that Arsène Lupin was christened. Arsène Lupin was armed and ready to fight, but without the means and authority to succeed, he was then only an apprentice in a profession in which he soon became a master.

With what joy he remembered the invitation he had received that evening! At last he had achieved his goal! At last he had undertaken a task worthy of his strength and skill! The Imbert millions! What a glorious feast for an appetite like his!

He had dressed up especially for the occasion: a shabby frock coat, baggy trousers, a frayed silk hat, a worn collar and cuffs, all quite correct in form, but with the unmistakable stamp of poverty. His tie was a black ribbon with a fake diamond attached. Thus dressed, he descended the stairs of the house where he lived in Montmartre. On the third floor, without stopping, he knocked on a closed door with the tip of his cane. He walked toward the outer boulevards. A streetcar car passed by. He got on, and someone who had followed him took a seat beside him. It was the lodger who occupied the room on the third floor. A moment later, this man said to Lupin:

"Well, sir?"

"Well, it's all settled."

"How?"

"I'm going there for breakfast."

"You're having breakfast ... there!"

"Certainly. Why not? I saved Monsieur Ludovic Imbert from certain death at your hands. Monsieur Imbert is not devoid of gratitude. He invited me to breakfast."

There was a brief silence. Then the other said:

"But you will not abandon the plan?"

"My dear boy," said Lupin, "when I arranged this little case of assault, when I took the trouble at three o'clock in the morning to beat you with my stick and kick you with my boot, at the risk of injuring my only friend, it was not my intention to forego the advantages that would accrue from a rescue so well arranged and executed. Oh, no, not at all."

"But the strange rumors one hears about her fortune?"

"Never mind that. For six months I have been engaged in this affair, investigating it, studying it, questioning the servants, the moneylenders and straw men; for six months I have shadowed the man and the woman. Consequently, I know what I am talking about. Whether the fortune came from old Brawford, as they claim, or from some other source, I don't care. I know it is a reality, that it exists. And one day it will be mine."

"Golly! One hundred million!"

"Let's say ten, or even five - that's enough! You've got a vault full of bonds, and it'll cost the devil if I don't get my hands on them."

The tramcar stopped at the Place de l'Etoile. The man whispered to Lupin:

"What do you want me to do now?"

"Nothing, for the moment. You will hear from me. There's no need to hurry." Five minutes later, Arsène Lupin climbed the magnificent staircase in the Imbert mansion, and Monsieur Imbert introduced him to his wife. Madame Gervaise Imbert was a small, plump woman and very talkative. She gave Lupin a warm welcome.

"I wished for us to meet to celebrate our savior," she said.

From the beginning, they treated "our savior" like an old and cherished friend. By the time dessert was served, their friendship was solidified and private confidences were exchanged. Arsène told the story of his life, his father's life as a magistrate, the sorrows of his childhood, and his present difficulties. Gervaise, for her part, told of her youth, her marriage, the kindness of old Brawford, the hundred millions she had inherited, the obstacles that prevented her from enjoying her inheritance, the funds she had had to borrow at an exorbitant rate of interest, her endless quarrels with Brawford's nephew and the lawsuits, the injunctions ... in fact, everything!

"Just think, Monsieur Lupin, the bonds are there, in my husband's office, and if we redeem a single coupon, we lose everything! They are there, in our safe, and we dare not touch them."

Monsieur Lupin shuddered at the very idea of having so much wealth near him. But he was sure that Monsieur Lupin would never be in the same predicament as his beautiful hostess, who declared that she dared not touch the money.

"Ah! they are here!" he repeated to himself; "they are here!"

A friendship formed under such circumstances soon led to closer relations. Upon discreet interrogation, Arsène Lupin confessed his poverty and need. Immediately the unfortunate young man was appointed private secretary to the Imberts couple, with a salary of one hundred francs a month. He was to come to the house every day and receive instructions for his work, and a room on the second floor was set aside as his office. This room was directly above Monsieur Imbert's office.

Arsène soon realized that his position as secretary was essentially a sinecure. In the first two months, he had only four important letters to copy and was called to Monsieur Imbert's office only once; consequently, he had the opportunity to formally inspect Imbert's safe only once. He also noticed that the secretary was not invited to the employer's social occasions. But he did not complain, preferring to remain modestly in the shadows and maintain his calm and freedom.

However, he did not waste time. From the beginning, he made clandestine visits to Monsieur Imbert's office and paid his respects to the safe, which was hermetically sealed. It was a huge block of iron and steel, cold and austere in appearance, impossible to crack with the ordinary tools of the burglar's trade. But Arsène Lupin was not discouraged.

"Where force fails, cunning wins," he said to himself. "The most important thing is to be on the spot when the opportunity arises. In the meantime, I must watch and wait."

He immediately made some preparations. After careful probing on the floor of his room, he inserted a lead pipe that penetrated at one point through the ceiling of Monsieur Imbert's office at a point between the two screeds of the cornice. Through this pipe he hoped to see and hear what was going on in the room below.

From then on, he spent his days at full length on the floor. Often he saw the Imberts holding a consultation in front of the safe, examining books and papers. When they turned the combination lock, he tried to learn the numbers and the number of turns they made to the right and left. He watched their movements; he tried to catch their words. There was also a key that was necessary to complete the opening of the safe. What were they doing with it? Did they hide it?

One day he saw them leave the room without locking the safe. He quickly descended the stairs and bravely entered the room. But they were already back.

"Oh! I beg your pardon," he said, "I made a mistake about the door."

"Come in, Monsieur Lupin, come in," cried Madame Imbert, "are you not at home here? We want your advice. Which bonds shall we sell? The foreign securities or the government bonds?"

"But the injunction?" said Lupin in surprise.

"Oh! It doesn't apply to all bonds."

She opened the door of the safe and took out a package of bonds. But her husband protested.

"No, no, Gervaise, it would be foolish to sell the foreign bonds. They are going up while the annuities are as high as they will ever be. What do you think, my dear friend?"

The dear friend had no opinion; yet he advised sacrificing the annuities. Then she pulled out another packet and took from it a paper. It proved to be a three percent annuity worth two thousand francs. Ludovic put the packet of bonds in his pocket. That afternoon, accompanied by his secretary, he sold the annuities to a stockbroker and realized forty-six thousand francs.

Whatever Madame Imbert might have said about it, Arsène Lupin did not feel at home in the Imbert house. On the contrary, his position there was a very special one. He learned that the servants did not even know his name. They called him monsieur. Ludovic always spoke of him in the same way, "You will say Monsieur. Is Monsieur here yet?" Why this mysterious form of address?

Moreover, after their first outburst of enthusiasm, the Imberts rarely spoke to him, and although they treated him with the consideration due a benefactor, they paid him little or no attention. They seemed to regard him as an eccentric character who did not want to be disturbed, and they respected his isolation as if it were a strict rule on his part. Once, while walking through the vestibule, he heard Madame Imbert say to the two gentlemen:

"He is such a barbarian!"

"Very well," he said to himself, "I am a barbarian."

And without attending to the question of their strange behavior, he went on with the execution of his own plans. He had decided not to rely either on chance or on the carelessness of Madame Imbert, who carried the key to the safe with her and, in locking it, always happened to twist the letters that formed the combination for the lock. Consequently, he had to act himself.

Finally, an incident occurred that accelerated the matter; it was the vehement campaign waged by some newspapers against the Imberts, accusing them of fraud. Arsène Lupin was present at some family conferences when this new misfortune was discussed. He decided that if he waited any longer, he would lose everything. During the next five days, he locked himself in his room instead of leaving the house around six o'clock, as was his habit. It was assumed he had gone out. But he lay on the floor looking at Monsieur Imbert's office. During these five evenings the favorable occasion he expected did not take place. He left the house about midnight by a side door to which he had the key.

But on the sixth day he learned that the Imberts, driven by the malicious insinuations of their enemies, intended to make an inventory of the contents of the safe.

"They'll do it tonight," Lupin thought.

And indeed, after dinner, Imbert and his wife retired to the office and began to examine the account books and the securities in the safe. Thus passed one hour after another. He heard the servants go upstairs to their rooms. There was no one on the second floor now. Midnight! The Imberts were still at work.

"I've got to get to work," Lupin muttered.

He opened his window. It opened onto a courtyard. Outside, everything was dark and silent. He took a knotted rope from his desk, attached it to the balcony outside his window, and quietly descended to the window below, which was that of Imbert's office. He stood motionless on the balcony for a moment, his ear attentive and his eye watchful, but the heavy curtains effectively hid the interior of the room. Carefully he pushed open the double window. If no one had noticed, it should give way at the slightest pressure, for he had fastened the latch during the afternoon in such a way that it could not penetrate the clasp.

The window gave way at his touch. Then, with infinite care, he pushed it open enough for his head to get in. He pushed the curtains a few inches apart, looked in, and caught sight of Monsieur Imbert and his wife sitting in front of the safe, deep in their work and talking quietly to each other at infrequent intervals.

He calculated the distance between him and them, considered the exact movements he would have to make to overcome them one by one before they could call for help, and was about to rush upon them when Madame Imbert said:

"Ah! the room is getting quite cold. I am going to bed now. And you, my dear?"

"I'll stay here and finish up."

"Finish up?! That will take all night."

"Not at all. An hour at the most."

She withdrew. Twenty minutes, thirty minutes passed. Arsène pushed the window open a little more. The curtains trembled. He pushed once more. Monsieur Imbert turned, and seeing that the curtains were blown by the wind, he got up to close the window.

There was no scream, not a trace of a struggle. In a few precise moments, and without causing him the slightest injury, Arsène stunned him, wrapped the curtain around his head, bound him hand and foot, and did all this in such a way that Monsieur Imbert had no opportunity to recognize his assailant.

He quickly approached the safe, seized two parcels which he tucked under his arm, left the office and opened the servants' gate. A carriage was waiting in the street.

"Take this first - and follow me," he said to the coachman. He returned to the office, and in two trips they emptied the safe. Then Arsène went to his own room, removed the rope and all other traces of his clandestine work.

A few hours later, Arsène Lupin and his assistant examined the stolen goods. Lupin was not disappointed, for he had foreseen that the Imberts' fortune was greatly exaggerated. It did not consist of hundreds of millions, not even tens of millions. Nevertheless, it was a very handsome sum, and Lupin expressed satisfaction.

"Of course," he said, "there will be a considerable loss when we have to sell the bonds, since we will have to dispose of them secretly at reduced prices. In the meantime, they will rest quietly in my desk, waiting for an opportune moment."

Arsène saw no reason why he should not go to Imbert's house the next day. But a glance at the morning papers revealed this startling fact: Ludovic and Gervaise Imbert had disappeared.

When the lawmen seized the safe and opened it, they found inside what Arsène Lupin had left behind - nothing.

These are the facts; and I learned the continuation of them one day when Arsène Lupin was in a confidential mood. He was pacing back and forth in my room, with a nervous step and a feverish look that was unusual for him.

"After all," I said to him, "it was your most successful venture."

Without giving a direct answer, he said:

"There are some impenetrable mysteries connected with this affair; some obscure points beyond my comprehension. For example: What was the cause of their escape? Why didn't they take advantage of the help I unknowingly gave them? It would have been so easy to say: `The hundred million were in the safe. They are no longer there because they were stolen.'"

"They lost their nerve."

"Yes, that's it - they lost their nerve ... On the other hand, it's true ... "

"What's true?"

"Oh! Nothing."

What was the meaning of Lupin's reticence? It was quite obvious that he had not told me everything; there was something he did not want to say. His behavior made me wonder. It had to be a very serious matter indeed to make a man like Arsène Lupin hesitate even for a moment. I randomly threw a few questions into the room.

"Have you seen her since?"

"No."

"And have you never felt the slightest degree of pity for these unfortunate people?"

"I!" he exclaimed with an outcry.

His sudden agitation astonished me. Had I touched him on a sore spot? I continued:

"Certainly. If you had not left them alone, they could have met the danger, or at least escaped with their pockets full."

"What do you mean?" he said indignantly. "I suppose you have some idea that my soul should be filled with remorse?"

"Call it remorse or regret ... whatever you like ... "

"You're not worth it."

"Have you no regret or remorse for stealing your fortune?"

"What assets?"

"The packages of bonds from her safe."

"Oh! I stole her bonds, did I? I robbed them of some of their assets? Is that my crime? Ah! My dear boy, you don't know the truth. You never imagined that those bonds were not worth the paper they were written on. Those bonds were false, they were counterfeit, every one of them, do you understand? THEY WERE COUNTERFEIT!"

I looked at him, dumbfounded.

"Forgeries! The four or five million?"

"Yes, counterfeit!" he exclaimed in a fit of anger. "Just a lot of scraps of paper! I couldn't even redeem a sou for all those bills! And you ask me if I have any remorse. They are the ones who should have remorse and pity.

They took me for a simpleton, and I fell into their trap. I was their last victim, their dumbest seagull!"

He was affected by genuine anger - the result of malice and wounded pride. He continued:

"From beginning to end, I got the worst of it. Do you know what part I played in this affair, or rather what part I was made to play? That of André Brawford! Yes, my boy, that is the truth, and I never suspected it. Only afterwards, while reading the newspapers, did it dawn on my stupid brain. While I posed as his 'rescuer,' as the gentleman who had risked his life to rescue Monsieur Imbert from the clutches of a murderer, they passed me off as Brawford. Wasn't that fabulous? This eccentric individual who had a room on the second floor, this barbarian who could only be seen from a distance, was Brawford, and Brawford was me! Thanks to me and the confidence I inspired under the name of Brawford, they were able to borrow money from the bankers and other money lenders. Ha! What an experience for a beginner! And I swear to you that I learned from that lesson!"

He stopped, grabbed my arm and said to me in a tone of exasperation:

"My dear friend, at this moment Gervaise Imbert owes me fifteen hundred francs."

I could not help laughing, so grotesque was his rage. He was making a mountain out of a molehill. The next moment he laughed himself and said:

"Yes, my boy, fifteen hundred francs. You must know that I had not received one sou of my promised salary, and on top of that they had borrowed from me the sum of fifteen hundred francs. All my youthful savings! And do you know why? To devote the money to charity! Let me tell you the whole story. She wanted it for some poor people she was supporting without her husband knowing about it. And my hard-earned money was snatched away by this silly pretext! Isn't that amusing? Arsène Lupin, cheated out of 1,500 francs by the lady from whom he stole four million! And how much time, patience and cunning I had to spend to achieve this result! It was the first time in my life that I was made a fool of, and I freely confess that I was downright robbed then, and cleanly!"

The Black Pearl

A heavy ringing woke the concierge of number nine, Avenue Hoche. She tugged grumblingly at the door cord:

"I thought everyone was already here. It must be three o'clock!"

"Maybe it's someone for the doctor," her husband muttered.

"Third floor, on the left. But the doctor doesn't go out at night."

"I guess he had to go tonight."

The visitor entered the vestibule, went up to the second floor, to the second, to the third, and without stopping at the doctor's door, he went on to the fifth floor. There he tried two keys. One of them fitted the lock.

"Ah! good!" he murmured, "that simplifies matters wonderfully. But before I start work, I had better prepare my retreat. Let me see ... have I had time enough to wake the doctor and be dismissed by him? Not yet ... a few minutes more."

After ten minutes, he descended the stairs and loudly grumbled about the doctor. The concierge opened the door for him and heard it click behind him. But the door did not close, for the man had quickly put a piece of iron into the lock in such a way that the bolt could not penetrate. Then, unnoticed by the concierge, he re-entered the house. In case of an alarm his retreat was assured. Silently, he climbed once more to the fifth floor. In the anteroom, by the light of his electric lantern, he laid his hat and coat on one of the chairs, took a seat on another, and covered his heavy shoes with felt slippers.

"Whew! Here I am - and how easy it was! I wonder why more people don't take up the lucrative and enjoyable profession of burglar. With a little care and thought, it becomes a most delightful profession. Not too quiet and monotonous, of course, for then it would become tiresome."

He unfolded a detailed plan of the apartment.

"Let me begin by getting my bearings. Here I see the vestibule where I sit. On the street front, the drawing room, the boudoir, and the dining room. It is useless to waste time there, because it seems that the Countess has deplorable taste ... not a jewel of any value! ... Well, let's get down to business! ... Ah! Here is a corridor; it must lead to the bedchambers. At ten feet I should come upon the door of the closet connected with the Countess's chamber."

He folded up his plan, extinguished his lantern, and walked down the corridor, counting the distance:

"One meter ... two meters ... three meters ... Here is the door ... My God, how simple it is! Only a small, simple latch now separates me from the chamber, and I know that the latch is exactly one meter and forty-three centimeters from the floor. So, thanks to a small cut I'm about to make, I can soon get rid of the bolt."

He took the necessary instruments out of his pocket. Then an idea occurred to him:

"Suppose the door happens to be unlocked. I'll try it first."

He turned the knob, and the door opened.

"My brave Lupin, luck is certainly with you ... Now what is to be done? You know the location of the rooms, you know the place where the Countess hides the black pearl. So to secure the black pearl, you simply have to be quieter than silence, more invisible than darkness itself."

Arsène Lupin spent half an hour trying to open the second door - a glass door that led to the Countess's bedchamber. But he managed it with so much skill and care that even if the Countess had been awake, she would not have heard the slightest noise. According to the plan of the rooms he had in his hands, he only had to pass by an armchair and then by a small table near the bed. On the table was a box of stationery, and in this box was hidden the black pearl.

He bent down and carefully crept across the carpet, following the outline of the recliner. When he reached the end of the chair, he stopped to suppress the pounding of his heart. Although no feeling of anxiety moved him, it was impossible for him to overcome the nervous restlessness usually felt in the midst of a profound silence. This circumstance astonished him, for he had passed through many more solemn moments without the slightest trace of emotion. No danger threatened him. Why, then, was his heart thumping like an alarm bell? Was it this sleeping woman who touched him? Was it the nearness of another pulsating heart?

He listened and thought he could perceive the rhythmic breathing of a sleeping person. It gave him confidence, like the presence of a friend. He searched and found the armchair; then, with slow, careful movements, he approached the table and groped with his outstretched arm in front of him. His right hand had touched one of the feet of the table. Ah! now he had only to stand up, take the pearl, and escape. This was fortunate, for his heart leaped in his breast like a wild beast, and made so much noise that he feared to awaken the Countess. With a tremendous effort of will he suppressed the wild thumping of his heart and was about to rise from the floor when his left hand came upon an object lying on the floor which he recognized as a candlestick - an overturned candlestick. A moment later, his hand came across another object: a clock - one of those small, leather-covered traveling clocks.

What had happened? He could not understand. This candlestick, this clock; why were these objects not in their usual place? What had happened in the terrible silence of the night?

Suddenly a cry escaped him. He had touched a strange, unspeakable thing! "No! no!" he thought, "it cannot be. It is a fantasy of my excited brain." For twenty or thirty seconds he remained motionless and terrified, his forehead drenched with perspiration, and in his fingers he still felt the terrible touch.

With a desperate effort he dared to stretch out his arm again. Once again his hand met that strange, unspeakable thing. He felt it. He had to feel it and find out what it was. He found that it was hair, human hair, and a human face; and that face was cold, almost icy.

However terrible the circumstances, a man like Arsène Lupin controls himself and controls the situation once he learns what it is. So Arsène Lupin quickly brought his lantern to bear. In front of him lay a woman covered in blood. Her neck and shoulders were covered with gaping wounds. He bent over her and examined her more closely. She was dead.

"Dead! Dead!" he repeated with a stunned expression.

He stared at the staring eyes, the grim mouth, the pale flesh, and the blood - all the blood that had flowed across the carpet and congealed there in thick, black stains. He rose and switched on the electric light. Then he caught sight of all the traces of a desperate struggle. The bed was in a state of great disorder. On the floor the candlestick and the clock, whose hands showed twenty minutes past eleven, farther away an overturned chair, and everywhere was blood, bloodstains, and pools of blood.

"And the black pearl?" he muttered.

The box of stationery was in place. He opened it eagerly. The jewelry box was there, but it was empty.

"Damn!" he muttered. "You have boasted of your good fortune far too soon, my friend Lupin. Now that the Countess is cold and dead and the black pearl is gone, the situation is anything but pleasant. Get out of here as soon as possible, or you will be in serious trouble."

But he did not move.

"Get out of here? Yes, of course. That's what any man would do, except Arsène Lupin. He has better things to do. Well, to proceed in an orderly fashion. In any case, your conscience is clear. Suppose you were the police chief and you were conducting an investigation into this matter ... it would take a clear head. Mine is a mess! "

He slumped into a chair, his clenched fists pressed against his burning forehead.

The murder in the Avenue Hoche is one of those which have lately surprised and puzzled the Parisian public, and I would certainly never have mentioned the matter if the veil of mystery had not been lifted by Arsène Lupin himself. No one knew the exact truth in this case.

Who did not know-because he had met her in the Bois-the beautiful Léotine Zalti, the once famous singer, wife, and widow of Count d'Andillot; the Zalti whose luxury dazzled all Paris some twenty years ago; the Zalti who gained a European reputation by the splendor of her diamonds and pearls?

It was said that she carried on her shoulders the capital of several banking houses and the gold mines of numerous Australian companies. Skilled jewelers worked for Zalti as they had once worked for kings and queens. And who does not remember the catastrophe in which all this wealth was swallowed up? Nothing remained of all the wonderful collection except the famous black pearl. The black pearl! That is, a fortune, if she had wanted to part with it.

But she preferred to keep it, to live in an ordinary apartment with her companion, her cook and a servant, than to sell this priceless jewel. There was a reason for it; a reason she was not afraid to reveal: the black pearl was the gift of an emperor! Nearly ruined and reduced to a most mediocre existence, she remained faithful to the companion of her happy and brilliant youth. The black pearl never left her possession. She wore it during the day and hid it at night in a place known only to her.

All these facts, published in the columns of the public press, served to stimulate curiosity; strange that the arrest of the alleged murderer only complicated the questions. Two days later, the newspapers published the following announcement:

We have been informed of the arrest of Victor Danègre, the servant of the Countess d'Andillot. The evidence against him is clear and convincing. Several bloodstains were discovered on the shiny sleeve of his livery vest, which Chief Inspector Dudouis found in his garret between the mattresses of his bed. In addition, a fabric-covered button was missing from this garment, and this button was found under the victim's bed.

"It is believed that Danègre, instead of going to his own room after dinner, slipped into the closet and saw through the glass door how the Countess hid the precious black pearl. This is merely a theory for which there is no evidence yet. There is one more obscure point. At seven o'clock in the morning Danègre went to the tobacco store on the Boulevard de Courcelles; both the porter and the shopkeeper confirm this fact. On the other hand, the Countess's companion and the cook, who sleeps down the hall, both state that when they got up at eight o'clock, the door of the anteroom and the door of the kitchen were locked. These two people have been in the service of the Countess for twenty years and are above suspicion. The question is: How did Danègre leave the apartment? Did he have another key? These are questions that the police will investigate.

In fact, the police investigation did not shed any light on the mystery. It was learned that Victor Danègre was a dangerous criminal, a drunkard and a debauchee. But as the investigation progressed, the mystery intensified and new oddities emerged. First, a young woman, Mademoiselle de Sinclèves, the Countess's cousin and sole heiress, explained that the Countess had written a letter to her a month before her death describing the way the black pearl had been hidden. The letter had disappeared the day after it was received. Who had stolen it?

Again, the concierge told how she had opened the door to a person who had asked for Doctor Harel. When questioned, the doctor testified that no one had rung his doorbell. Then who was this person? And an accomplice?

The theory of an accomplice was then adopted by the press and the public, but also by Ganimard, the famous inspector.

"Lupin is behind this affair," he told the judge.

"Pha!" the judge exclaimed, "you have Lupin on the brain. You see him everywhere."

"I see him everywhere because he is everywhere."

"You'd better say you see him every time you come across something you can't explain. Besides, you overlook the fact that the crime was committed at twenty minutes past eleven in the evening, as the clock shows, while the nocturnal visit mentioned by the concierge took place at three in the morning."

Judicial officers often form a hasty conviction of a suspect's guilt and then distort all subsequent discoveries to conform to their established theory. The deplorable record of Victor Danègre, a habitual criminal, drunkard, and libertine, influenced the judge, and despite the fact that nothing new was discovered to confirm the initial clues, his official opinion remained firm and unshaken. He concluded his investigation, and a few weeks later the trial began.

The process proved to be slow and protracted. The judge was listless, and the prosecutor presented the case in a careless manner. Under these circumstances, Danègre's defense attorney had an easy task. He pointed out the flaws and inconsistencies in the indictment and argued that the evidence was totally insufficient to convict the defendant. Who had made the key, the indispensable key without which Danègre could not have locked the door behind him when leaving the apartment? Who had ever seen such a key, and what had become of it? Who had seen the murderer's knife, and where is it now?

"In any event," argued the prisoner's defense attorney, "the prosecution must prove beyond a reasonable doubt that the prisoner committed the murder. The prosecution must prove that the mysterious person who entered the house at three o'clock in the morning is not the guilty party. Sure, the clock read eleven o'clock. But what does that prove? I submit that it proves nothing. The murderer could turn the hands of the clock to any hour and thus deceive us as to the exact time of the crime."

Victor Danègre was acquitted.

He left prison at dusk on a Friday, weakened and depressed by six months of imprisonment. The investigation, the solitude, the trial, and the deliberations of the jury had filled him with terror. At night he was plagued by terrible nightmares and haunted by eerie visions of the scaffold. He was a mental and physical wreck.

Under the assumed name of Anatole Dufour, he rented a small room on the heights of Montmartre and lived off odd jobs wherever he could find them. He led a miserable existence. Three times he got regular employment, only to be recognized and then dismissed. Sometimes he suspected that men were following him - no doubt policemen who wanted to trap him and denounce him. He could almost feel the strong hand of the law grabbing him by the collar.

One evening, as he was having dinner in a neighboring restaurant, a man came in and sat down at the same table. He was about forty years old and wore a frock coat of dubious cleanliness. He ordered a soup, vegetables, and a bottle of wine. After he had eaten his soup, he fixed his eyes on Danègre and looked at him intently. Danègre winced. He was sure that this was one of the men who had been following him for several weeks. What did he want? Danègre tried to rise, but he could not. His limbs refused to carry him. The man poured himself a glass of wine and then filled Danègre's glass. The man raised his glass and said:

"To your health, Victor Danègre."

Victor winced in shock and stammered:

"I ... I ... no, no ... I swear to you ... "

"You swear what? That you are not yourself? The servant of the countess?"

"What servant? My name is Dufour. Ask the owner."

"Yes, Anatole Dufour for the owner of this restaurant, but Victor Danègre for the officers of the law."

"That's not true! Someone lied to you."

The newcomer pulled a card from his pocket and handed it to Victor, who read on it:

Grimaudan, ex-inspector of the Criminal Investigation Department.

Private business.

Victor shuddered as he said:

"You are connected with the police?"

"No, not now, but I have a liking for the business, and I continue to pursue it in a more profitable way. From time to time I come across a golden opportunity - like your case."

"My case?"

"Yes, yours. I assure you it is a promising one, provided you are inclined to be reasonable."

"But if I am not reasonable?"

"Oh, my good friend, you are in no position to refuse me anything I ask."

"What is it ... what do you want?" stammered Victor anxiously.

"Well, I will tell you in a few words. I am sent by Mademoiselle de Sinclèves, the heiress of the Countess d'Andillot."

"What for?"

"To recover the black pearl."

"Black pearl?"

"The one you stole."

"But I don't have it."

"You have it."

"If I had it, I would be the murderer."

"You are the murderer."

Danègre flashed a forced smile.

"Fortunately for me, monsieur, the court disagreed with you. The jury was unanimous in its verdict of acquittal. And when a man has a clear conscience and twelve good men speak for him ... "

The ex-inspector grabbed him by the arm and said:

"No pretty speeches, my boy. Listen to me and weigh my words carefully. You will see they are worth considering. Now, Danègre, three weeks before the murder you stole the cook's key to the servants' door and had a duplicate made, by a locksmith named Outard, 244 rue Oberkampf."

"That's a lie!" growled Victor. "No man has seen this key. There is no such key."

"Here it is."

After a silence Grimaudan continued:

"You killed the Countess with a knife you bought the same day at the Bazar de la Republique, where you also ordered the duplicate key. It has a triangular blade with a groove running from end to end."

"This is all nonsense. You're just guessing about something you don't know. No one has ever seen the knife."

"Here it is."

Victor Danègre flinched. The ex-inspector continued:

"There are some rust stains on it. Would you like me to tell you how they got there?"

"Well ... you have a key and a knife. Who can prove they are mine?"

"The locksmith and the clerk you bought the knife from. I have already refreshed their memory, and when you come face to face with them, they will inevitably recognize you."

His speech was dry and hard, with a tone of firmness and precision. Danègre trembled with fear, and yet he strove desperately to maintain an appearance of indifference.

"Is that all the evidence you have?"

"Oh no, not at all. I have much more. For instance, after the crime you went out the same way you came in. But in the middle of the dressing room, seized by a sudden fear, you leaned against the wall to support yourself."

"How do you know that? No one can know such a thing," argued the distraught man.

"The police, of course, don't know anything about it. They'd never think of lighting a candle and examining the walls. But if they had, they would have found a faint red stain on the white plaster, but quite clearly the imprint of your blood-wet thumb, which you had pressed against the wall. Now, as you know, according to the Bertillon system, thumbprints are one of the most important means of identification."

Victor Danègre was pale; large drops of sweat rolled down his face and fell on the table. He stared with a wild look at the strange man who had told the story of his crime as faithfully as if he had been an invisible witness to it. Overwhelmed and powerless, Victor bowed his head. He felt that it was useless to fight this man. So he said:

"How much will you give me if I give you the pearl?"

"Nothing."

"Oh, you're joking! Or do you mean that I should give you an object worth thousands and hundreds of thousands and get nothing in return?"

"You will get your life. Is that nothing?"

The unhappy man shuddered. Then Grimaudan added in a milder tone:

"Come, Danègre, this pearl has no value in your hands. It is quite impossible to sell it; so what is the use of your keeping it?"

"There are pawnbrokers ... and one day I will be able to get something for it."

"But that day may be too late."

"Why?"

"Because you might be in the hands of the police by then, and with the evidence I can provide-the knife, the key, the thumbprint-what will become of you?"

Victor propped his head on his hands and thought. He felt that he was lost, irrevocably lost, and at the same time a feeling of fatigue and depression overcame him. He murmured softly:

"When do I have to give it to you?"

"Tonight ... in an hour."

"And if I refuse?"

"If you refuse, I will send this letter to the prosecutor; in this letter Mademoiselle de Sinclèves denounces you as the murderer."

Danègre poured two glasses of wine, which he drank in rapid succession, then rose and said:

"Pay the bill, and let us go. I've had enough of this cursed business."

Night had fallen. The two men walked down Rue Lepic and followed the outer boulevards toward Place de l'Etoile. They continued their way in silence; Victor had a stooped gait and a downcast face. When they reached the Parc Monceau, he said:

"We are near the house."

"You left the house only once before your arrest, and that was to go to the tobacco store."

"Here it is," Danègre said in a muffled voice.

They walked along the garden wall of the Countess's house and crossed a street, at the corner of which was the tobacco store. A few steps farther on Danègre stopped, his limbs trembling, and he sank down on a bench.

"Well-what now?" asked his companion.

"It's there."

"Where? Now come, don't make mischief!"

"There - in front of us."

"Where?"

"Between two paving stones."

"Which one?"

"Look."

"Which stones?"

Victor made no reply.

"Ah, I see!" exclaimed Grimaudan, "you want me to pay for the information."

"No ... but ... I am afraid that I will starve."

"So, that's why you're hesitating? Well, I'm not going to be hard on you. How much do you want?"

"Enough to buy a ticket to America."

"All right."

"And a hundred francs to get me through until I find work there."

"You shall have two hundred. Now, speak."

"Count the paving stones to the right of the manhole. The bead is between the twelfth and the thirteenth."

"In the gutter?"

"Yes, near the sidewalk."

Grimaudan glanced around to see if anyone was looking. A few streetcars passed by and there were a few pedestrians, but they won't suspect anything. He opened his pocket knife and put it between the twelfth and thirteenth stones.

"What if it's not there?" he said to Victor.

"It has to be there, unless someone saw me bend down and hide it."

Could it be that the black pearl had been tossed into the gutter dirt to be picked up by the first person who passed by? The black pearl - a fortune!

"How far down?" he asked.

"About ten inches."

He dug up the wet earth. The tip of his knife hit something. He enlarged the hole with his finger. Then he pulled the black bead from its dirty hiding place.

"Good! Here are your two hundred francs. I will send you the ticket to America."

The next day this article appeared in the Echo de France and was picked up by the leading newspapers all over the world:

Yesterday the famous black pearl came into the possession of Arsène Lupin, who took it from the murderer of the Countess d'Andillot. Facsimiles of this precious jewel will soon be exhibited in London, St. Petersburg, Calcutta, Buenos Ayres and New York.

Arsène Lupin will gladly consider all proposals made to him through his agents.

"And so crime is always punished and virtue rewarded," said Arsène Lupin, after telling me the preceding story of the black pearl.

"And so you, under the assumed name of Grimaudan, former detective inspector, were chosen by fate to deprive the criminal of the benefit of his crime."

"Exactly. And I confess that the affair gives me infinite satisfaction and pride. The forty minutes I spent in the Countess d'Andillot's apartment after I learned of her death were the most exciting and riveting moments of my life. During those forty minutes, when I was in a highly dangerous position, I calmly studied the crime scene and came to the conclusion that the crime must have been committed by one of the domestic servants. I also decided that this servant had to be arrested to get the pearl, so I left the button of the smock under the bed; it was also important for me to have convincing proof of his guilt, so I took the knife I found on the floor and the key I found in the lock. I closed and locked the door and wiped away the fingerprints on the plaster in the closet. In my opinion, it was one of those flashes of genius ... "

"Genius," I said, interrupting him.

" ... Of genius, if you will. But I'm flattered that it wouldn't have occurred to a mere mortal. To combine at once the two elements of the problem-an arrest and an acquittal; to use the formidable machinery of the law to crush and humiliate my victim, and to put him in a condition in which, if free, he would surely fall into the trap I set for him!"

"Poor devil ... "

"Poor devil, you say? Victor Danègre, the assassin! He could have descended into the deepest depths of vice and crime if he had kept the black pearl. Well, he's alive! Imagine that! Victor Danègre is alive!"

"And you have the black pearl."

He took it from one of the secret pockets of his wallet, examined it, looked at it tenderly, caressed it with loving fingers, and sighed as he said:

"What cold Russian prince, what vain and foolish rajah may one day possess this priceless treasure! Or perhaps some American millionaire, destined to become the owner of this piece of exquisite beauty, which once adorned the beautiful bosom of Leontine Zalti, the Countess d'Andillot."

Herlock Sholmes arrives too late

"It is truly remarkable, Velmont, what a great resemblance you bear to Arsène Lupin!"

"How do you know?"

"Oh! Like everyone else, from photographs, no two of which are alike, but each of which leaves the impression of a face ... something like yours ..."

Horace Velmont showed some annoyance.

"Quite so, my dear Devanne. And, believe me, you are not the first to have noticed it."

"It is so striking," Devanne insisted, "that if you had not been recommended to me by my cousin d'Estevan, and if you were not the famous artist whose beautiful seascapes I so admire, I would doubtless have warned the police of your presence in Dieppe."

This advance was met with an outburst of laughter. In the large dining room of the Château de Thibermesnil on this occasion, in addition to Velmont, were the following guests: Father Gélis, the parish priest, and a dozen officers whose regiments were quartered nearby and who had accepted the invitation of the banker Georges Devanne and his mother. One of the officers then remarked:

"I have heard that an accurate description of Arsène Lupin has been transmitted to all the police along the coast since his daring deed on the Paris-Havre express."

"I suppose so," said Devanne. "That was three months ago; and a week later I made the acquaintance of our friend Velmont at the Casino, and since then he has graced me with several visits-a pleasant prelude to a more serious visit which he will pay me some day-or rather one of these nights."

This speech evoked further laughter, and the guests then went into the old guardroom, a huge room with a high ceiling that took up the entire lower part of the Tour Guillaume, and in which Georges Devanne had collected the incomparable treasures that the lords of Thibermesnil had amassed over many centuries. It contained antique chests, credenzas, mantels and chandeliers. The stone walls were hung with magnificent tapestries. The deep embrasures of the four windows were fitted with benches, and the Gothic windows consisted of small panes of colored glass set in a leaden frame. Between the door and the window to the left stood a huge Renaissance-style bookcase, on the pediment of which was emblazoned in gold letters the word Thibermesnil and below it the proud family crest: "Fais ce que veulx ". When the guests had lit their cigars, Devanne resumed the conversation.

"And remember, Velmont, you have no time to lose; in fact, tonight is the last chance you will have."

"How so?" asked the painter, who seemed to think the matter a joke. Devanne was about to reply when his mother bade him be silent, but the excitement of the occasion and the desire to interest his guests urged him to speak.

"Bah!" he muttered. "I can say it now. It will do no harm."

The guests drew nearer, and he began to speak with the satisfied air of a man who has an important announcement to make.

"Tomorrow afternoon at four o'clock Herlock Sholmes, the famous English detective for whom there is no such thing as mystery, Herlock Sholmes, the most remarkable puzzle-solver the world has ever known, that wonderful man who seems like a creation of a romantic novelist- Herlock Sholmes will be my guest!"

Immediately Devanne was the target of numerous eager questions. "Is Herlock Sholmes really coming?" "Is it that serious?" "Is Arsène Lupin really in these parts?"

"Arsène Lupin and his gang are not far away. In addition to the robbery of Baron Cahorn, the thefts in Montigny, Gruchet, and Crasville are attributed to him."

"Did he send you a warning, as he did Baron Cahorn?"

"No," Devanne replied, "he cannot use the same trick twice."

"What then?"

"I will show you."

He rose and pointed to a small gap between the two huge tomes on one of the shelves of the bookcase:

"There was once a book there-a sixteenth-century book called Chronique de Thibermesnil, which contained the history of the castle since it was built by Duke Rollo on the site of an earlier feudal fortress. In the book there were three engraved plates; one of them was a general view of the whole estate; another the plan of the buildings; and the third - I would like to draw your attention to it in particular - the third was the sketch of an underground passage, the entrance to which is outside the first line of the fortress walls, while the other end of the passage is here, in this room. Now, this book disappeared a month ago."

"Hell!" said Velmont, "that looks bad. But it doesn't seem a sufficient reason to send for Herlock Sholmes."

"Certainly it was not sufficient in itself, but another incident has occurred which gives special significance to the disappearance of the book. There was another copy of this book in the National Library in Paris, and the two books differed in certain details concerning the subterranean passage; for example, each contained drawings and annotations which were not printed but written in ink and more or less obliterated. I knew these facts, and I knew that the exact location of the passage could only be determined by comparing the two books. Now, the day after my book disappeared, the book was sought in the National Library by a reader who carried it away, and no one knows how the theft came about."

The guests uttered exclamations of surprise.

"Certainly, the matter looks serious," said one.

"Well, the police have investigated the matter and, as usual, have found no clue."

"They never do when Arsène Lupin is involved."

"Exactly; and so I decided to ask for help from Herlock Sholmes, who agreed to get in touch with Arsène Lupin."

"What glory for Arsène Lupin!" said Velmont. "But if our national thief, as he is called, has no evil intentions against your castle, Herlock Sholmes will have made his journey in vain."

"There are other things that will interest him, such as the discovery of the underground passage."

"But you told us that one end of the passage is outside the fortress walls and the other inside this room!"

"Yes, but in which part of the room? The line representing the passage on the maps ends here, with a small circle marked with the letters T.G., which undoubtedly stand for Tour Guillaume. But the tower is round, and who can tell exactly where the passageway touches the tower?"

Devanne lit a second cigar and poured himself a glass of Bénédictine. His guests pestered him with questions, and he was pleased with the interest his remarks had generated. Then he continued:

"The secret is lost. No one knows it. Legend has it that the former lords of the castle passed the secret from father to son on their deathbeds until Geoffroy, the last of the line, was beheaded during the Revolution in his nineteenth year."

"That was over a century ago. Surely someone has been looking for him since then?"

"Yes, but they haven't found it. After I bought the castle, I searched diligently for it, but to no avail. You must remember that this tower is surrounded by water and connected to the castle only by a bridge; consequently, the passage must be below the old moat. The plan that was in the book in the National Library showed a series of stairs with a total of forty-eight steps, indicating a depth of more than ten meters. You see, the secret lies within the walls of this room, and yet I don't want to tear them down."

"Is there nothing to indicate where it is?"

"Nothing."

"Monsieur Devanne, we should turn our attention to the two quotations," suggested Father Gélis.

"Oh!" exclaimed Monsieur Devanne, laughing, "our worthy Father likes to read memoirs and rummage in the musty archives of the chateau. Anything to do with Thibermesnil interests him greatly. But the quotes he cites only serve to complicate the mystery. He read somewhere that two kings of France knew the key to the riddle."

"Two kings of France? Who were they?"

"Henry the Fourth and Louis the Sixteenth. And the legend goes like this: On the eve of the Battle of Arques, Henry the Fourth spent the night in this castle. At eleven o'clock in the evening, Louise de Tancarville, the most beautiful woman in Normandy, was brought into the castle through the underground passage by Duke Edgard, who at the same time informed the king about the secret passage. Afterwards the king entrusted the secret to his minister Sully, who in his turn tells the story in his book 'Royales Oeconomies d'État ', without commenting on it, but connecting it with the incomprehensible sentence: `Turn one eye on the bee that trembles, the other eye will lead to God!'"

After a brief silence, Velmont laughed and said:

"Certainly, that does not throw a blinding light on the subject."

"No; but Father Gélis maintains that Sully hid the key to the secret in that strange phrase, in order to keep the secret from the secretaries to whom he dictated his memoirs."

"That's an ingenious theory," said Velmont.

"Yes, and perhaps it is nothing more; I cannot see that it throws any light on the mysterious enigma."

"And was it also to receive the visit of a lady that Louis the Sixteenth caused the passage to be opened?"

"I do not know," said Monsieur Devanne. "All I can say is that the king stopped here one night in 1784, and that the famous iron casket found in the Louvre contained a paper bearing these words in the king's handwriting: 'Thibermesnil 3-4-11. ' "

Horace Velmont laughed heartily and exclaimed:

"At last! And now that we have the magic key, where is the man who can put it in the invisible lock?"

"Laugh all you like, Monsieur," said Father Gélis, "but I am convinced that the solution is contained in these two sentences, and some day we shall find a man who can interpret them."

"Herlock Sholmes is the man," said Monsieur Devanne, "unless Arsène Lupin beats him to it. What is your opinion, Velmont?"

Velmont rose, put his hand on Devanne's shoulder, and declared:

"I think that the information provided by your book and the National Library book was deficient in a very important detail, which you have now provided. I thank you for that."

"What is it?"

"The missing key. Now that I have it, I can get right to work," Velmont said.

"Of course; without wasting a minute," said Devanne, smiling.

"Not even a second!" replied Velmont. "Tonight, before the arrival of Herlock Sholmes, I must sack your castle."

"You have no time to lose. Oh! By the way, I can drive you over tonight."

"To Dieppe?"

"Yes. I am meeting Monsieur and Madame d'Androl and a young lady of their acquaintance, who will arrive on the midnight train."

Devanne then turned to the officers and added:

"Gentlemen, I expect to see you all tomorrow at breakfast."

The invitation was accepted. The company dispersed, and a few moments later Devanne and Velmont sped off in an automobile toward Dieppe. Devanne dropped the artist off in front of the casino and drove to the train station. At twelve o'clock his friends got off the train. Half an hour later, the automobile was in front of the entrance to the chateau. At one o'clock, after a light supper, they retired. The lights were extinguished, and the castle was enveloped in the darkness and silence of the night.

The moon shone through a gap in the clouds and filled the salon with its bright white light. But only for a moment. Then the moon withdrew again behind its ethereal curtain, and darkness and silence reigned. No sound was heard, only the monotonous ticking of the clock. It struck two and then endlessly repeated the seconds. Then, three o'clock.

Suddenly something clicked, like the opening and closing of a signal disc warning a passing train. A thin beam of light flashed into every corner of the room, like an arrow leaving a trail of light behind it. It shot from the central fluting of a column that supported the pediment of the bookcase. Like a glittering circle of polished silver, it rested for a moment on the opposite panel, then flashed in all directions like a guilty eye scrutinizing every shadow. It disappeared for a short time, but burst forth again as an entire section of the bookcase spun on an axis, revealing a large opening like a vault.

A man entered, carrying an electric lantern. He was followed by a second man carrying a pulley and various tools. The leader inspected the room, listened in for a moment, and said:

"Call the others."

Then eight men, burly fellows with determined faces, entered the room and immediately began removing the furniture. Arsène Lupin moved quickly from one piece of furniture to another, examining each, and depending on its size or artistic value, he instructed his men to take it or leave it. If the order was given to take it, it was carried to the gaping tunnel mouth and ruthlessly thrust into the bowels of the earth. Such was the fate of six armchairs, six small Louis XV chairs, a quantity of Aubusson tapestries, some candlesticks, paintings by Fragonard and Nattier, a bust of Houdon, and some statuettes. Sometimes Lupin would linger in front of a beautiful chest or a magnificent painting and sigh:

"This is too heavy ... too big ... what a pity!"

In forty minutes the room was dismantled; and it had been accomplished as neatly and with as little noise as if the various items had been packed and wrapped for the occasion.

Lupin said to the last man, who removed through the tunnel:

"You need not come back. You understand that as soon as the wagon is loaded, you will go to the barn at Roquefort?"

"But you, patron?"

"Leave me the motorcycle."

When the man had disappeared, Arsène Lupin pushed the part of the bookcase back into place, carefully covered the traces of the man's footsteps, opened a door, and entered a gallery that was the only connection between the tower and the castle. In the center of this gallery was a glass case that had caught Lupin's attention. It contained a valuable collection of clocks, snuff boxes, rings, and miniatures of rare and beautiful workmanship. He broke open the lock with a small crowbar and felt great pleasure in touching these gold and silver ornaments, these exquisite and delicate works of art.

He carried with him a large canvas sack specially prepared for the removal of such knickknacks. He filled it. Then he filled the pockets of his coat, vest and trousers. And he was about to place a row of beaded necklaces over his left arm when he heard a soft sound. He listened. No, he was not fooled. The sound persisted. Then he remembered that at one end of the gallery was a staircase leading to an unoccupied apartment, but probably occupied that night by the young lady Monsieur Devanne had brought with his other visitors from Dieppe.

Immediately he extinguished his lantern, and had scarcely gained the friendly shelter of a window parapet when the door at the top of the stairs was opened, and a faint light illuminated the gallery. He could feel - for hidden by a curtain he could not see - a woman walking cautiously down the upper steps of the staircase. He hoped she would not come any closer. But she continued to descend and even came a little way into the room. Then she uttered a faint cry. No doubt she had discovered the broken and dismantled closet.

She advanced again. Now he could smell the perfume and hear the pounding of her heart as she approached the window behind which he was hiding. She came so close that her skirt brushed the window curtain, and Lupin sensed that behind her, in the shadows, she suspected the presence of another within reach of her hand. He thought, "She is afraid. She'll go away." But she did not go. The candle she held in her trembling hand grew brighter. She turned, hesitated a moment, seemed to listen, then suddenly drew aside the curtain.

They were face to face. Arsène was taken aback. He murmured, involuntarily:

"You ... you ... Mademoiselle."

It was Mademoiselle Nelly. Miss Nelly! his fellow traveler on the transatlantic steamer, whom he had dreamed of on that memorable voyage, who had witnessed his arrest, and who, instead of betraying him, had thrown into the water the Kodak in which he had hidden the banknotes and diamonds. Miss Nelly! that lovely creature whose memory of her face had sometimes exhilarated, sometimes saddened the long hours of captivity.

It was so unexpected a meeting that brought them together in this castle at this hour of the night that they could neither move nor utter a word; they were amazed, mesmerized, each of them by the sudden appearance of the other. Trembling with emotion, Miss Nelly staggered to a seat. He stopped in front of her.

Gradually he comprehended the situation and imagined the impression he must have made at that moment with his arms laden with knickknacks and his pockets overflowing with loot and a canvas bag. Confusion overcame him, and he actually blushed at finding himself in the position of a thief caught in the act. To them, from now on, he was a thief, a man who puts his hand in someone else's pocket, who enters houses and robs people while they sleep.

A watch fell to the floor, then another. More objects followed, slipping out of his hand one by one. Then, driven by a sudden decision, he dropped the other items into an armchair, emptied his pockets and unpacked his bag. Feeling very uncomfortable in Nelly's presence, he stepped toward her, intending to address her, but she shuddered, rose quickly, and fled in the direction of the parlor. The doorman closed behind her. He followed her. She stood trembling and astonished at the sight of the desolate room. He said to her at once:

"Tomorrow, at three o'clock, everything will be returned. The furniture will be returned."

She made no reply, so he repeated:

"I promise. Tomorrow, at three o'clock. Nothing in the world could make me break that promise ... Tomorrow, at three o'clock."

There followed a long silence, which he dared not break, while the young girl's excitement evoked in him a feeling of sincere regret. Quietly, without a word, he turned away, thinking, "I hope she goes away. I can't bear her presence." But the young girl suddenly began to stammer:

"Listen ... footsteps ... I hear someone ... "

He looked at her in amazement. She seemed overwhelmed by the thought of approaching danger.

"I don't hear anything," he said.

"But you must go - you must escape!"

"Why should I go?"

"Because - you must. Oh! Don't stay here a minute longer. Go!"

She ran quickly to the door leading to the gallery and listened. No, there was no one there. Perhaps the noise was outside. She waited a moment, then returned reassured.

But Arsène Lupin had disappeared.

As soon as Monsieur Devanne learned of the ransacking of his castle, he said to himself: It was Velmont who did it, and Velmont is Arsène Lupin. This theory explained everything, and there was no other plausible explanation. And yet the idea seemed absurd to him. It was ridiculous to suppose that Velmont was anyone other than Velmont, the famous artist and clubmate of his cousin d'Estevan. When the captain of the gendarmerie arrived to investigate the matter, Devanne did not even think to mention his absurd theory.

Throughout the morning, the chateau was bustling with activity. The gendarmes, the local police, the chief of police of Dieppe, the villagers, all ran back and forth in the halls, examining every nook and cranny that presented itself. The approach of the maneuvering troops, the rattling fire of muskets, added to the picturesque character of the scene.

The first search revealed no clue. Neither on the doors nor on the windows were there any signs of a break-in. Consequently, the removal of the goods must have taken place through the secret passage. However, there was no evidence of footprints on the floor or any unusual marks on the walls.

Investigation, however, revealed a curious fact that pointed to the whimsical character of Arsène Lupin: the famous sixteenth-century chronicle had been restored to its accustomed place in the library, and beside it lay a similar book that was none other than the volume stolen from the National Library.

At eleven o'clock the officers arrived. Devanne greeted them with his usual cheerfulness; for however much the loss of his art treasures might grieve him, his great wealth enabled him to bear the loss philosophically. His guests, Monsieur and Madame d'Androl and Mademoiselle Nelly, were introduced; and then it was noticed that one of the expected guests had not come. It was Horace Velmont. Would he come? His absence had reawakened Monsieur Devanne's suspicions. But at twelve o'clock he arrived. Devanne exclaimed:

"Ah! There you are!"

"Why, am I not on time?" asked Velmont.

"I am but you may not be ... after such a busy night. I suppose you know the news?"

"What news?"

"They have robbed the castle."

"Nonsense!" exclaimed Velmont, smiling.

"Just as I predicted. But first accompany Miss Underdown to the dining room. Mademoiselle, permit me ... "

He paused as he noticed the young girl's extreme excitement. Then, recalling the incident, he said:

"Ah! Of course, you met Arsène Lupin on the steamer, before his arrest, and you are amazed at the resemblance. Is that it?"

She did not answer. Velmont stood before her and smiled. He bowed. She took his outstretched arm. He escorted her to her seat and took a seat opposite her. During breakfast, the conversation turned exclusively to Arsène Lupin, the stolen goods, the secret passage, and Herlock Sholmes. Only at the end of the meal, when the conversation had moved on to other topics, did Velmont join in. Then he was alternately amused and serious, talkative and thoughtful. And all his remarks seemed to be directed toward the young girl. But she, quite absorbed, did not seem to hear them.

Coffee was served on the terrace overlooking the main courtyard and the French garden in front of the main facade. The regimental band played on the lawn, and crowds of soldiers and peasants wandered through the park.

Miss Nelly had not for a moment forgotten Lupin's solemn promise: "Tomorrow at three o'clock everything will be returned."

At three o'clock! And the hands of the big clock in the right wing of the castle now showed twenty minutes to three. Involuntarily her eyes wandered to the clock every minute. She also watched Velmont, who was quietly rocking back and forth in a comfortable rocking chair.

Ten minutes to three! ... Five minutes to three! ... Nelly was impatient and anxious. Was it possible that Arsène Lupin would keep his promise at the appointed hour, when the castle, the courtyard and the park were full of people and the lawmen were just carrying out their investigations? And yet ... Arsène Lupin had made his solemn promise to her. "It will be just as he said," she thought, so deeply impressed was she by the authority, the energy, and the certainty of this remarkable man. It no longer seemed to her like a miracle, but, on the contrary, like a natural event that had to occur in the normal course of things. She blushed and turned her head.

Three o'clock! The big clock struck slowly: one ... two ... three ... Horace Velmont took out his watch, looked at it and put it back in his pocket. A few seconds passed in silence; then the crowd in the courtyard parted to make way for two wagons that were just entering through the gate, each drawn by two horses. They were army wagons of the type used to transport provisions, tents, and other necessary military supplies. They stopped in front of the main entrance, and a sergeant jumped from one of the wagons and inquired for Monsieur Devanne. A moment later the latter came out of the house, descended the stairs, and beheld his furniture, pictures, and ornaments carefully packed and arranged under the tarpaulins of the carriages.

Upon questioning, the sergeant produced an order he had received from the officer of the day. In it, the second company of the fourth battalion was ordered to proceed to the crossroads of Halleux in the forest of Arques, collect the furniture and other objects deposited there, and deliver them at three o'clock to Monsieur Georges Devanne, the owner of the chateau of Thibermesnil. Signed: Colonel Beauvel.

"At the crossroads," the sergeant explained, "we found everything ready, lying on the grass, guarded by some passers-by. It seemed very strange, but orders were orders."

One of the officers examined the signature. He declared it a forgery; but a clever imitation. The wagons were unloaded and the goods returned to their place in the castle.

During this excitement Nelly had remained alone at the far end of the terrace, absorbed in confused and distracted thoughts. Suddenly she noticed Velmont approaching her. She would have wanted to avoid him, but the balustrade surrounding the terrace barred her retreat. She was cornered. She could not move. A ray of sunlight falling through the sparse foliage of a bamboo illuminated her beautiful golden hair. He addressed her in a low voice:

"Have I not kept my promise?"

Arsène Lupin stood close to her. No one else was near. He repeated in a calm, gentle voice:

"Did I not keep my promise of last night?"

He expected a word of thanks, or at least a slight movement that would betray her interest in fulfilling his promise. But she remained silent.

Her contemptuous attitude annoyed Arsène Lupin; and he realized the great distance that separated him from Miss Nelly now that she had learned the truth. Gladly would he have justified himself in her eyes, or at least pleaded extenuating circumstances, but he recognized the absurdity and futility of such an attempt. Finally, controlled by a surging tide of memories, he muttered:

"Ah! How long ago that was! Remember the long hours on the deck of the 'Provence'. At that time you carried a rose in your hand, a white rose like the one you carry today. I asked you for the rose. You pretended not to hear me. After you left, I found the rose - forgotten, no doubt - and kept it."

She made no reply. She seemed far away. He continued:

"Remembering those happy hours, forget what you know now. Separate the past from the present. Do not think of me as the man you saw last night, but look at me, if only for a moment, as you did in those distant days. Am I not the same?"

She raised her eyes and looked at him as he had asked. Then, without saying a word, she pointed to a ring he wore on his index finger. Only the ring was visible; but the setting, facing the palm, was of a magnificent ruby. Arsène Lupin blushed. The ring belonged to Georges Devanne. He smiled bitterly and said:

"You are right. Nothing can be done about it. Arsène Lupin is now and will always be Arsène Lupin. For you, he can no longer even be a memory. Forgive me, I should have known that any attention I give you now is an insult. Forgive me."

He stepped aside, hat in hand. Nelly passed in front of him. He was inclined to stop her and beg her pardon. But his courage deserted him, and he contented himself with following her with his eyes, as he had done when she went down the gangway to the pier in New York. She climbed the steps that led to the door and disappeared into the house. He did not see her again.

A cloud obscured the sun. Arsène Lupin stood looking at the prints of her little feet in the sand. Suddenly he winced. On the box of bamboo beside which Nelly had been standing, he saw the rose, the white rose he had wished for but dared not ask for. Forgotten, no doubt - her too! But how - on purpose or by distraction? He grasped it eagerly. Some of its petals fell to the ground. He picked them up, one by one, like precious relics.

"Come!" he said to himself, "I have nothing more to do here. I must think of my safety before Herlock Sholmes arrives."

The park was deserted, but some gendarmes were stationed at the park gate. He entered a grove of pines, jumped over the wall, and, taking a shortcut to the station, followed a path across the fields. After walking for about ten minutes, he came to a place where the path narrowed and ran between two steep banks. In this ravine he met a man walking in the opposite direction. It was a man about fifty years old, tall, clean shaven and wore clothes with a foreign cut. He carried a heavy cane and had a small bag strapped over his shoulder. When they met, the stranger spoke with a slight English accent:

"Excuse me, monsieur, is this the way to the castle?"

"Yes, monsieur, straight ahead, and when you reach the wall, turn left. They are waiting for you there."

"Ah!"

"Yes, my friend Devanne told us last night that you were coming, and I am glad to be the first to welcome you. Herlock Sholmes has no more ardent admirer than I."

There was a hint of irony in his voice that he quickly regretted, for Herlock Sholmes eyed him from head to toe with such a keen, penetrating gaze that Arsène Lupin felt as if he were being seized, captured, and registered by it, more thoroughly and precisely than he had ever experienced from a camera.

"My negative is now taken," he thought, "and it will be useless to use a disguise with this man. He would look right through it. But, I wonder, did he recognize me?"

They bowed to each other as if to part. But at that moment they heard the sound of horses' feet, accompanied by the clang of steel. It was the gendarmerie. The two men had to retreat to the embankment in the bushes to avoid the horses. The gendarmes moved past, but since they followed each other at a considerable distance, it took several minutes for them to pass. Lupin thought:

"It all depends on the question: Did he recognize me? If so, he will probably take advantage of the opportunity. It's a difficult situation."

When the last rider had passed, Herlock Sholmes stepped out and brushed the dust off his clothes. Then he and Arsène Lupin looked at each other for a moment, and if any one could have seen them at that moment it would have been an interesting sight, and memorable as the first meeting of two remarkable men, so strange, so powerfully equipped, both of superior quality, and destined by fate, by their peculiar qualities, to rush upon each other like two equal forces opposed by nature in the vastness of space.

Then the Englishman said, "I thank you, monsieur."

They parted. Lupin walked toward the station, and Herlock Sholmes continued on his way to the chateau.

The local officials had given up the investigation after several hours of unsuccessful effort, and the people at the chateau awaited the arrival of the English detective with lively curiosity. At first glance they were a little disappointed by his banal appearance, so different from the image they had formed of him. He in no way resembled the romantic hero, the mysterious and devilish personage, which the name of Herlock Sholmes had evoked in their imagination. But Monsieur Devanne exclaimed with pleasure:

"Ah! Monsieur, you are here! I am delighted to see you. It is a long-delayed pleasure. I hardly regret what has happened, for it gives me an opportunity to meet you. But, how did you come?"

"By train."

"But I sent my automobile to meet you at the station."

"An official reception, eh? With music and fireworks! Oh, no, not for me. That's not my way of doing business," grumbled the Englishman.

This speech unsettled Devanne, who replied with a forced smile:

"Fortunately, business has become much easier since I wrote to you."

"In what way?"

"The robbery took place last night."

"If you had not announced my visit, the robbery probably would not have been committed last night."

"When, then?"

"Tomorrow, or another day."

"And in that case?"

"Lupin would have been trapped," the detective said.

"And my furniture?"

"Would not have been carried away."

"Ah! But my things are here. They were returned at three o'clock."

"By Lupin."

"By two army wagons."

Herlock Sholmes put on his cap and adjusted his bag. Devanne exclaimed anxiously:

"But, monsieur, what are you going to do?"

"I'm going home."

"Why?"

"Your goods have been returned; Arsène Lupin is far away-there is nothing more for me to do."

"Yes, there is. I need your help. What happened yesterday may happen again tomorrow, because we don't know how he got in, how he escaped, and why he returned the goods a few hours later."

"Ah! You don't know ... "

The thought of a problem to be solved spurred Herlock Sholmes' interest.

"Very well, let us conduct a search - immediately - and alone, if possible."

Devanne understood and led the Englishman into the drawing room. In a dry, clear voice and in sentences that seemed to have been prepared in advance, Sholmes asked a series of questions about the events of the previous evening and also inquired about the guests and members of the household. He then examined the two volumes of the Chronique, compared the plans of the underground passage, asked for a repetition of the sentences Father Gélis had discovered, and then asked:

"Was that the first time you spoke those two sentences to anyone yesterday?"

"Yes."

"And you never communicated them to Horace Velmont?"

"No."

"Good, order the automobile. I have to leave in an hour."

"In an hour?"

"Yes; in that time Arsène Lupin will have solved the problem you set him."

"I ... set him the task ... "

"Yes, Arsène Lupin or Horace Velmont - it's the same thing."

"I thought so. Ah! The scoundrel!"

"Well, let's see," said Sholmes, "last night at ten o'clock you supplied Lupin with the information he was missing and had been seeking for many weeks. During the night he found time to solve the problem, gather his men, and rob the castle. I will be in just as much of a hurry."

He walked from one end of the room to the other, lost in thought, then sat down, crossed his long legs, and closed his eyes.

Devanne waited, rather embarrassed. He thought, "Is that man asleep? Or is he just meditating?" He left the room to give some instructions, and when he returned, he found the detective on his knees, examining the carpet at the foot of the stairs in the gallery.

"What's that?" he inquired.

"See ... there ... stains from a candle."

"You're right -and they're still quite fresh."

"And you'll also find them at the top of the stairs and around the closet that Arsène Lupin broke into and took the books from, which he then placed in this armchair."

"What do you conclude from that?"

"Nothing. These facts would undoubtedly explain the reason for the return, but that is a minor matter which I cannot pursue further. The main question is the secret passage. Tell me first, is there a chapel about two or three hundred yards from the castle?"

"Yes, a dilapidated chapel in which is the tomb of Duke Rollo."

"Tell your chauffeur to wait for us near this chapel."

"My chauffeur has not returned. If he had, they would have informed me. Do you think the secret passage leads to the chapel? What reason have - "

"I would ask you, monsieur," interrupted the detective, "to get me a ladder and a lantern."

"You need a ladder and a lantern?"

"Certainly, or I would not have asked for it."

Devanne, somewhat unsettled by this crude logic, rang the bell. The two items were brought with the rigor and precision of military orders.

"Place the ladder against the bookshelf, to the left of the word Thibermesnil."

Devanne placed the ladder as instructed, and the Englishman continued:

"More to the left ... to the right ... There! ... Now climb up ... All the letters are in relief, aren't they?"

"Yes."

"First turn the letter 'I' one way or the other."

"Which one? There are two of them."

"The first one."

Devanne picked up the letter and exclaimed:

"Ah! Yes, it turns to the right. Who told you that?"

Herlock Sholmes did not answer this question, but continued with his instructions:

"Now take the letter 'B'. Move it back and forth like a bolt."

Devanne did so, and to his great surprise, there was a clicking sound.

"That's right," Sholmes said. "Now we'll go to the other end of the word Thibermesnil, try the letter 'I' and see if it opens like a gate."

With some solemnity, Devanne grabbed the letter. It opened, but Devanne fell off the ladder, for the entire portion of the bookshelf that lay between the first and last letters of the word spun on an axis, revealing the underground passage.

Herlock Sholmes said coolly:

"You are not hurt?"

"No, no," Devanne said as he straightened up, "not hurt, just confused. I cannot understand now ... these letters turn ... the secret passage opens ..."

"Certainly. Does not this coincide exactly with the formula given by Sully? Point one eye to the bee that trembles, the other eye leads to God."

"But Louis the Sixteenth?" asked Devanne.

"Louis the Sixteenth was a skilled locksmith. I read a book he wrote about combination locks. It was a good idea of the owner of Thibermesnil to show his majesty a clever mechanism. As an aid to memory, the king wrote: 3-4-11, that is, the third, fourth and eleventh letters of the word."

"Exactly. That's clear to me. It explains how Lupin got out of the room, but not how he got in. And it's certain he came from the outside."

Herlock Sholmes lit his lantern and stepped into the passage.

"Look! The whole mechanism lies open here, like the work of a clock, and you can reach the back of the letters. Lupin operated the combination from this side-that's all."

"What proof is there of that?"

"Evidence? Why, look at the puddle of oil. Lupin anticipated that the wheels would need oiling."

"Did he know about the other entrance?"

"As far as I know," Sholmes said. "Follow me."

"Into this dark passage?"

"Are you afraid?"

"No, but are you sure you can find your way out?"

"With my eyes closed."

They descended twelve steps, then another twelve, and two more flights of twelve steps each. Then they went through a long corridor whose brick walls showed the marks of repeated restorations and dripped with water in some places. The earth was also very damp.

"We're going under the pond," Devanne said, a little nervously.

At last they came to a staircase with twelve steps, followed by three more with twelve steps each, which they climbed with difficulty, and then found themselves in a small cave cut into the rock. This was as far as they could go.

"Hell," muttered Sholmes, "nothing but bare walls. It's a provocation."

"Let's go back," Devanne said. "I've seen enough to be satisfied."

But the Englishman raised his eyes and heaved a sigh of relief. There he saw the same mechanism and the same word as before. He had only to work the three letters. He did, and a granite block swung out of place. On the other side, this granite block formed the tombstone of Duke Rollo, and the word "Thibermesnil" was engraved in relief. Now they were in the small ruined chapel, and the detective said:

"The other eye leads to God, that is, to the chapel."

"It is wonderful!" exclaimed Devanne, amazed at the clairvoyance and vividness of the Englishman. "Can it be that these few words were sufficient for you?"

"Bah!" declared Sholmes, "they weren't necessary at all. On the map in the National Library book, the drawing ends in a circle on the left, as you know, and in a cross on the right, as you don't know. Well, this cross must refer to the chapel in which we are now standing."

Poor Devanne could not believe his ears. It was all so new, so unfamiliar to him. He exclaimed:

"It is incredible, wondrous, and yet of a childlike simplicity! How is it that no one has ever solved the riddle?"

"Because no one has ever united the essential elements, that is, the two books and the two sentences. No one, except Arsène Lupin and myself."

"But Father Gélis and I knew all about these things, and so did ... " Sholmes smiled and said:

"Monsieur Devanne, not everyone can solve mysteries."

"I spent ten years trying to do what you did in ten minutes."

"Bah! I'm used to that."

They stepped out of the chapel and found an automobile.

"Ah! There's a car waiting for us."

"Yes, it's mine," said Devanne.

"Mine? You said your chauffeur had not returned."

They approached the machine, and Monsieur Devanne questioned the chauffeur:

"Eduard, who gave you the order to come here?"

"Well, it was Monsieur Velmont."

"Monsieur Velmont? Did you meet him?"

"Near the station, and he told me to come to the chapel."

"To come to the chapel! What for?"

"To wait for you, monsieur, and your friend."

Devanne and Sholmes exchanged glances, and Monsieur Devanne said:

"He knew the riddle would be an easy one for you. That is a fine compliment."

A smile of satisfaction lit up the detective's serious features for a moment. The compliment pleased him. He shook his head as he said:

"A clever man! I knew that when I saw him."

"Have you seen him?"

"I met him not long ago - on my way from the station."

"And you knew it was Horace Velmont - I mean, Arsène Lupin?"

"No, but I assumed it was him ... from a certain ironic speech he made."

"And you let him escape?"

"Of course I did. Although I had everything on my side, like five gendarmes passing us by."

"Damn it!" exclaimed Devanne. "You should have taken the opportunity."

"Really, monsieur," said the Englishman haughtily, "when I meet an adversary like Arsène Lupin, I don't take accidental chances, I create them."

But time was pressing, and since Lupin had been kind enough to send the automobile, they decided to take advantage of it. They got into the comfortable sedan, Eduard took his place at the wheel, and they drove toward the station. Suddenly Devanne's eyes fell on a small package in one of the car's pockets.

"Ah! What's that? A small parcel! Whose is it?"

"It's for you."

"For me?"

"Yes, it's addressed: Herlock Sholmes, from Arsène Lupin."

The Englishman took the package, opened it, and found that it contained a watch.

"Ah!" he exclaimed with an angry gesture.

"A watch," said Devanne. "How did it get there?"

The detective did not answer.

"Oh! It's your watch! Arsène Lupin is returning your watch! But to give it back, he must have taken it. Ah! I see! He took your watch! That's a good watch! Herlock Sholmes' watch, stolen by Arsène Lupin! My God! That's funny! Really ... you'll have to excuse me ... I can't help it."

He roared with laughter, unable to contain himself. Then he said in a tone of serious conviction:

"A clever man, indeed!"

The Englishman did not budge. On the way to Dieppe he did not speak a word, but stared at the flying landscape. His silence was terrible, unfathomable, fiercer than the wildest rage. At the station he spoke again calmly, but in a voice that told of the tremendous energy and willpower of this famous man. He said:

"Yes, he is a clever man, but one day, Monsieur Devanne, I will have the pleasure of placing the hand I am now extending to you on his shoulder. And I believe that one day Arsène Lupin and Herlock Sholmes will meet again. Yes, the world is too small - we will meet - we must meet - and then ... "

FIN

Printed in Great Britain
by Amazon